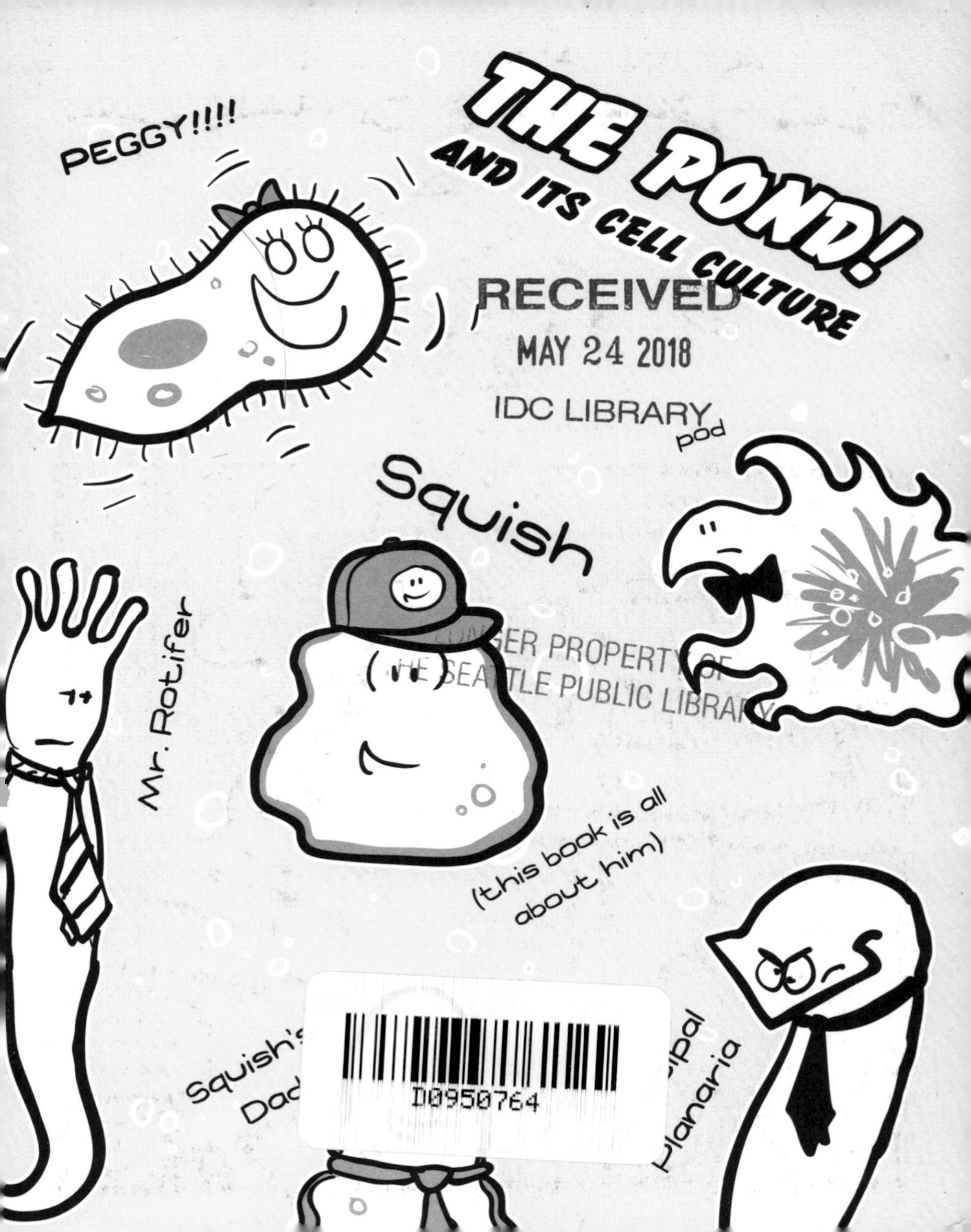
THE POND!
AND ITS CELL CULTURE
PEGGY!!!!
Squish
Mr. Rotifer
(this book is all about him)
Squish's
Dad
cipal
Planaria

Read ALL the SQUISH books!

#1 SQUISH: Super Amoeba
#2 SQUISH: Brave New Pond
#3 SQUISH: The Power of the Parasite
#4 SQUISH: Captain Disaster
#5 SQUISH: Game On!
#6 SQUISH: Fear the Amoeba

squish
GAME ON!

BY JENNIFER L. HOLM & MATTHEW HOLM

RANDOM HOUSE 🏠 NEW YORK

Published in the United States by Random House Children's Books, a division of Random House LLC, a Penguin Random House Company, New York.

Visit us on the Web! randomhousekids.com

Educators and librarians, for a variety of teaching tools, visit us at RHTeachersLibrarians.com

Library of Congress Cataloging-in-Publication Data
Holm, Jennifer L.
Game on! / by Jennifer L. Holm & Matthew Holm. —
1st ed. p. cm. — (Squish ; #5)
Summary: Squish the amoeba neglects his homework, parents, friends, and even his Super Amoeba comic books when he discovers the video game Mitosis.
ISBN 978-0-307-98299-5 (trade) —
ISBN 978-0-307-98300-8 (lib. bdg.) —
ISBN 978-0-307-98301-5 (ebook)
1. Graphic novels. [1. Graphic novels. 2. Amoeba—Fiction. 3. Video games—Fiction. 4. Cartoons and comics—Fiction. 5. Superheroes—Fiction.] I. Holm, Matthew. II. Title.
PZ7.7.H65Gam 2013 741.5'973—dc23 2012016421

MANUFACTURED IN MALAYSIA 12 11 10 9 8 7 6 5 4
First Edition

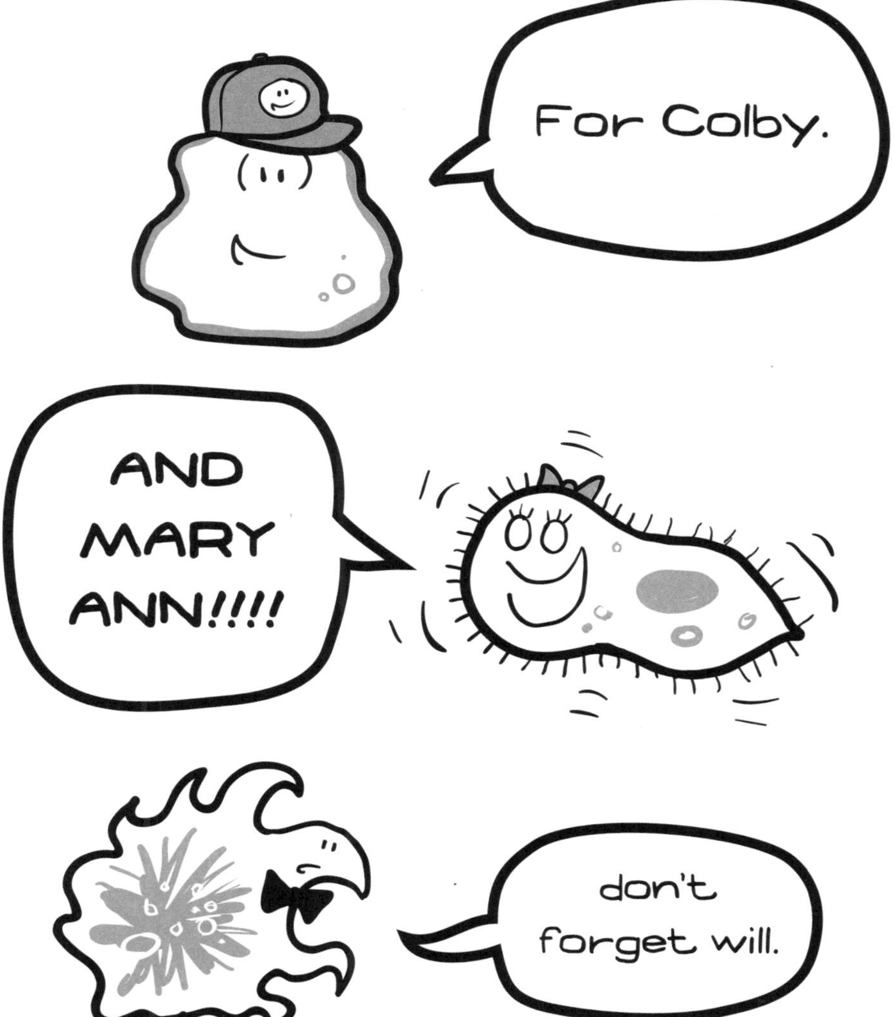
For Colby.
AND MARY ANN!!!!!
don't forget will.

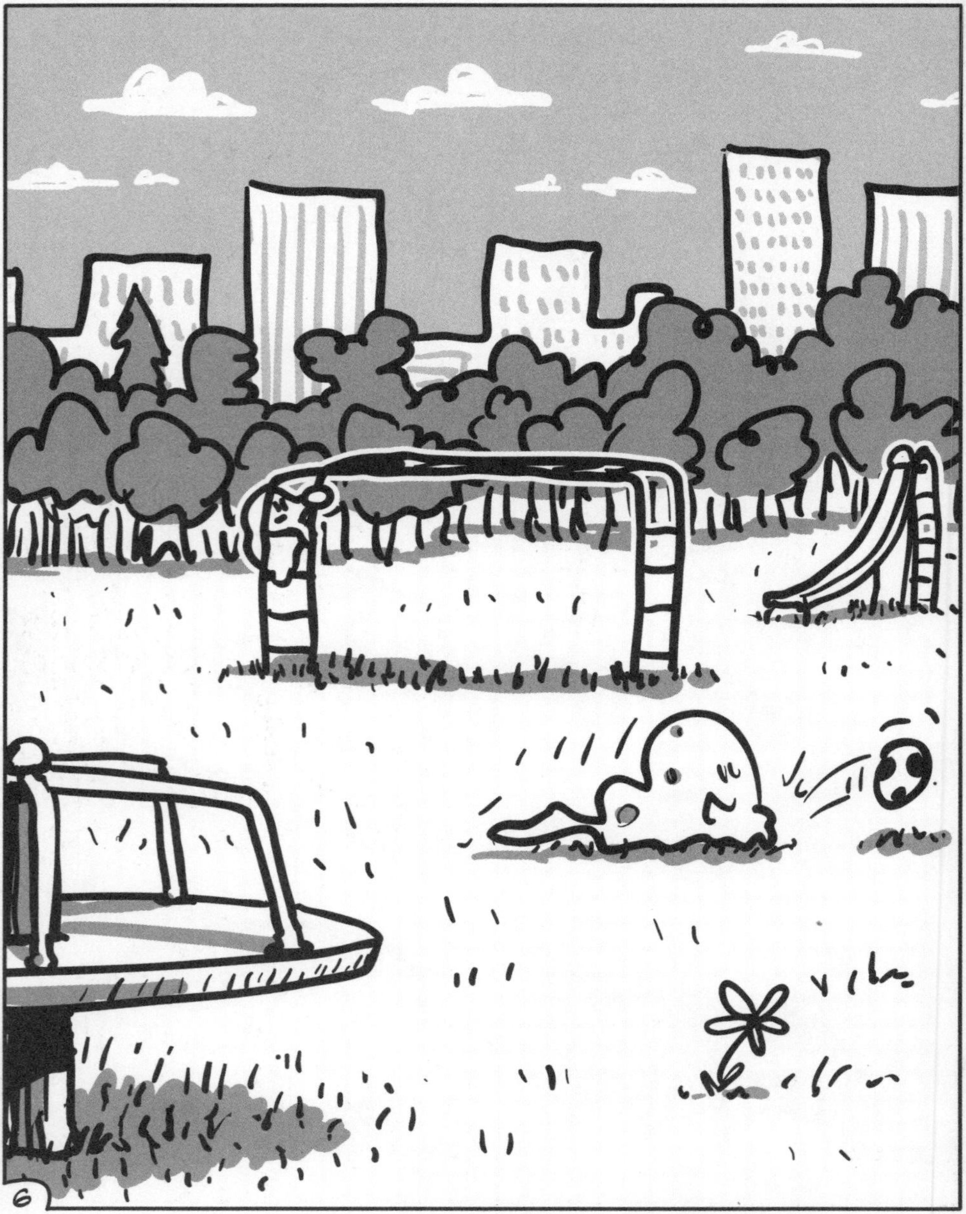

STRETCH
SLIP!
AGH!

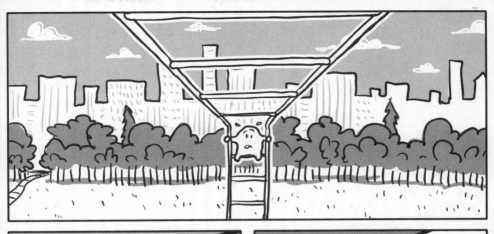

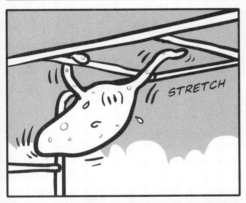

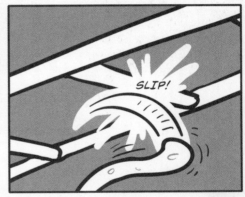

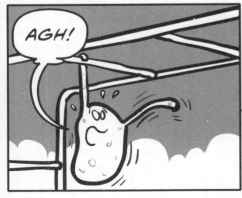

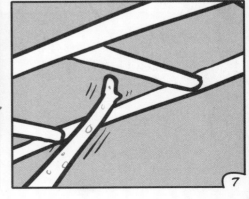

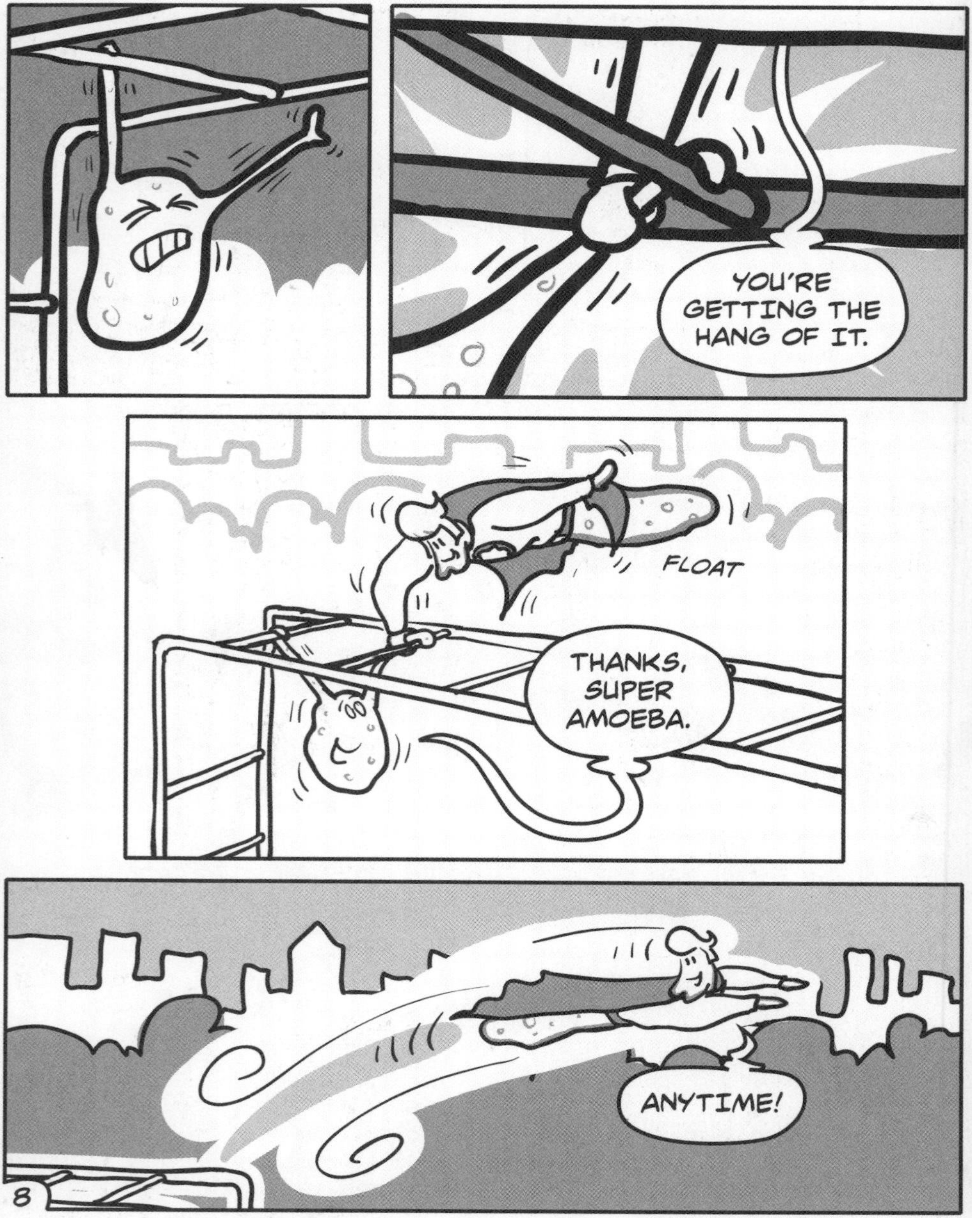
YOU'RE GETTING THE HANG OF IT.
FLOAT
THANKS, SUPER AMOEBA.
ANYTIME!

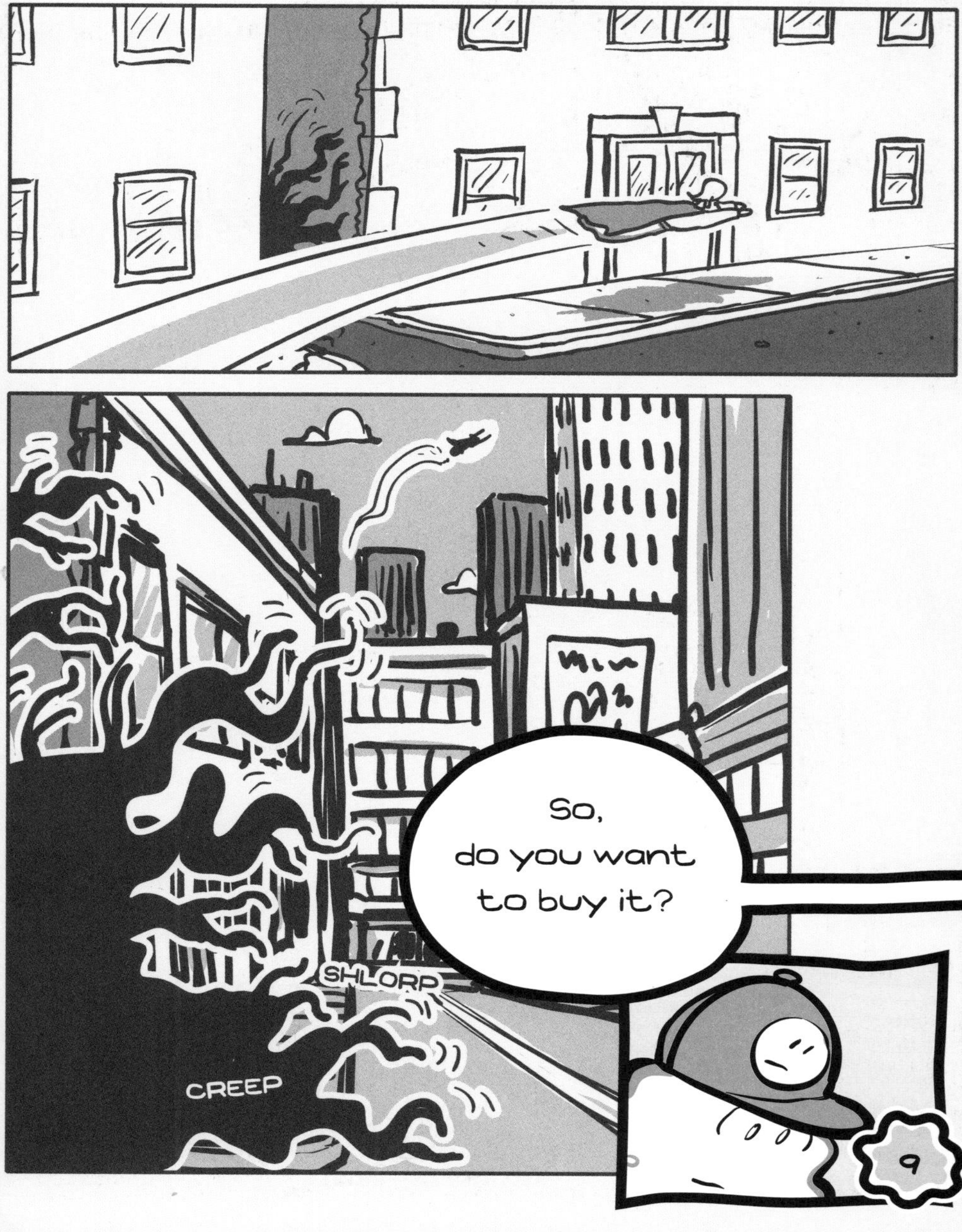
SHLORP
CREEP
So, do you want to buy it?

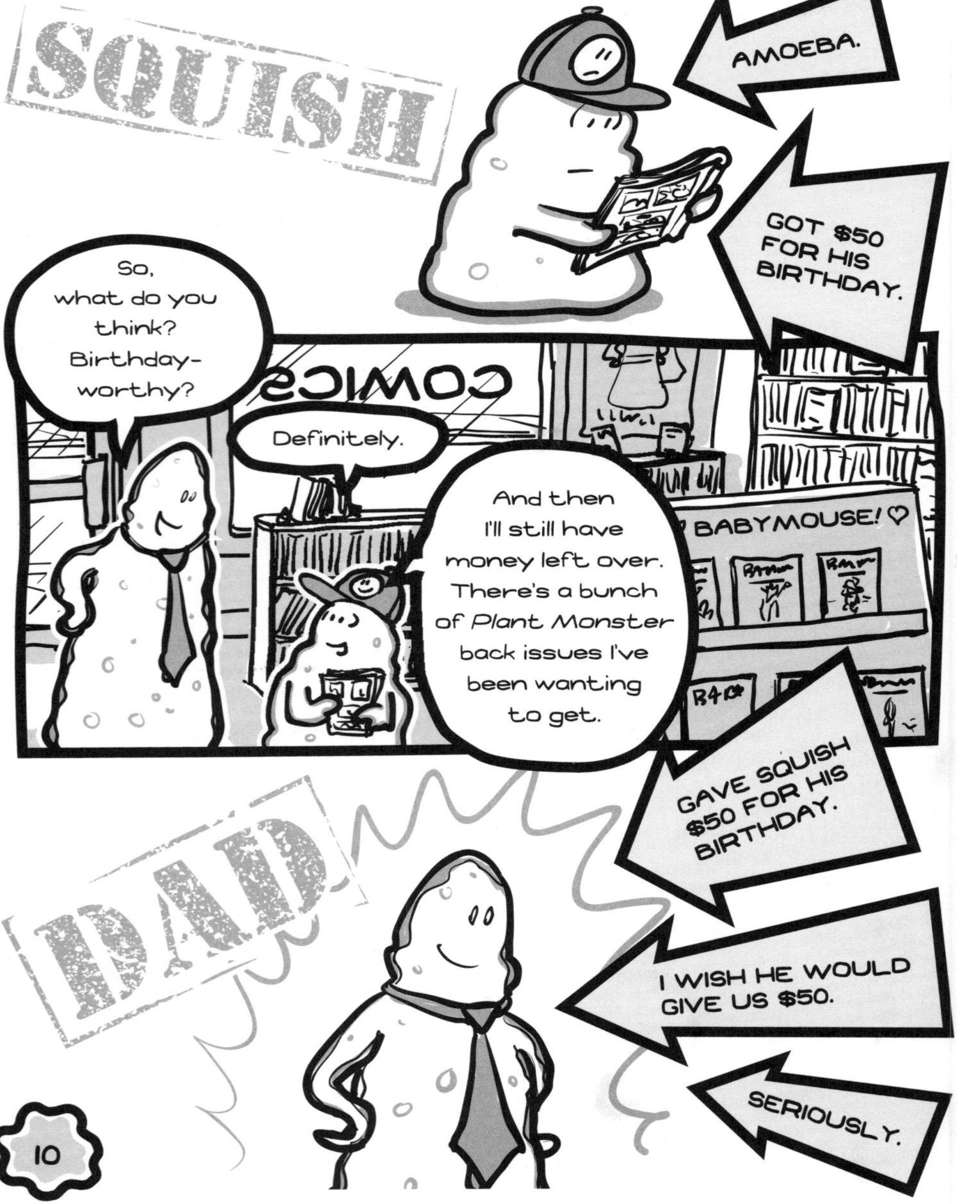
SQUISH
AMOEBA.
GOT $50 FOR HIS BIRTHDAY.
So, what do you think? Birthday-worthy?
Definitely.
And then I'll still have money left over. There's a bunch of *Plant Monster* back issues I've been wanting to get.
BABYMOUSE!
DAD
GAVE SQUISH $50 FOR HIS BIRTHDAY.
I WISH HE WOULD GIVE US $50.
SERIOUSLY.

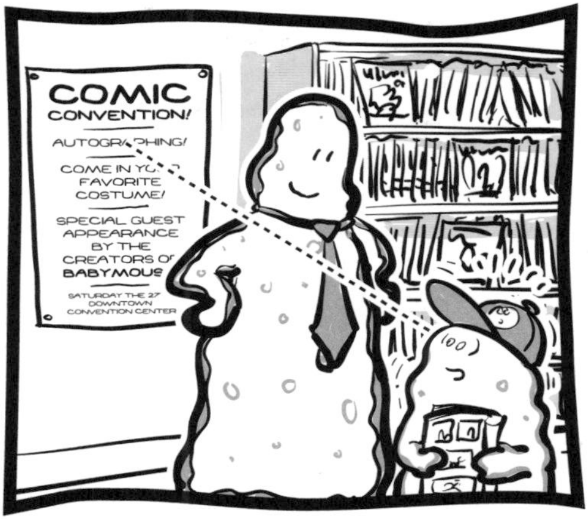
COMIC
CONVENTION!
SPECIAL GUEST
APPEARANCE
BY THE

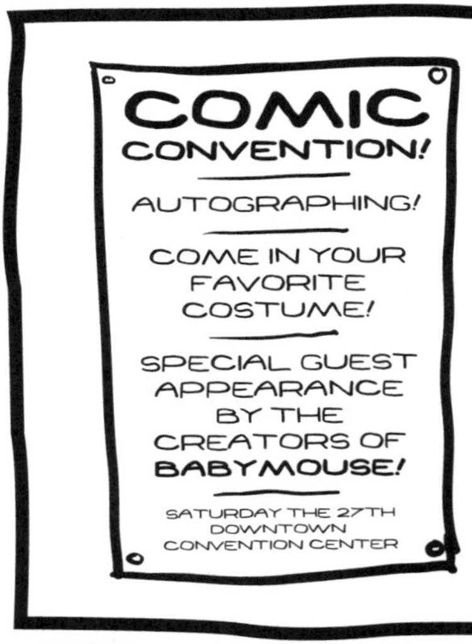
COMIC
CONVENTION!
AUTOGRAPHING!
COME IN YOUR
FAVORITE
COSTUME!
SPECIAL GUEST
APPEARANCE
BY THE
CREATORS OF
BABYMOUSE!
SATURDAY THE 27TH
DOWNTOWN
CONVENTION CENTER

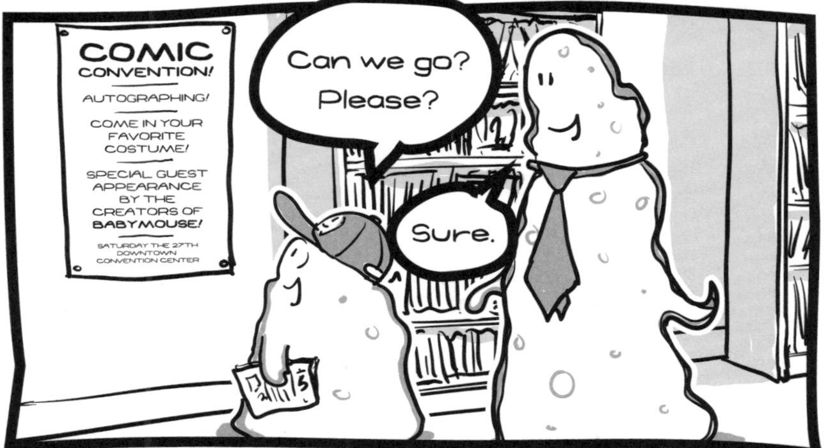
COMIC
CONVENTION!
AUTOGRAPHING!
COME IN YOUR
FAVORITE
COSTUME!
SPECIAL GUEST
APPEARANCE
BY THE
CREATORS OF
BABYMOUSE!
SATURDAY THE 27TH
DOWNTOWN
CONVENTION CENTER
Can we go?
Please?
Sure.

Want to dress up? I will if you will. . . .

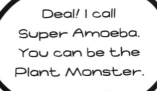

Deal! I call Super Amoeba. You can be the Plant Monster.

COMIC BOOK SHOP

The Plant Monster? Isn't he the one who looks like an asparagus?

Snicker.

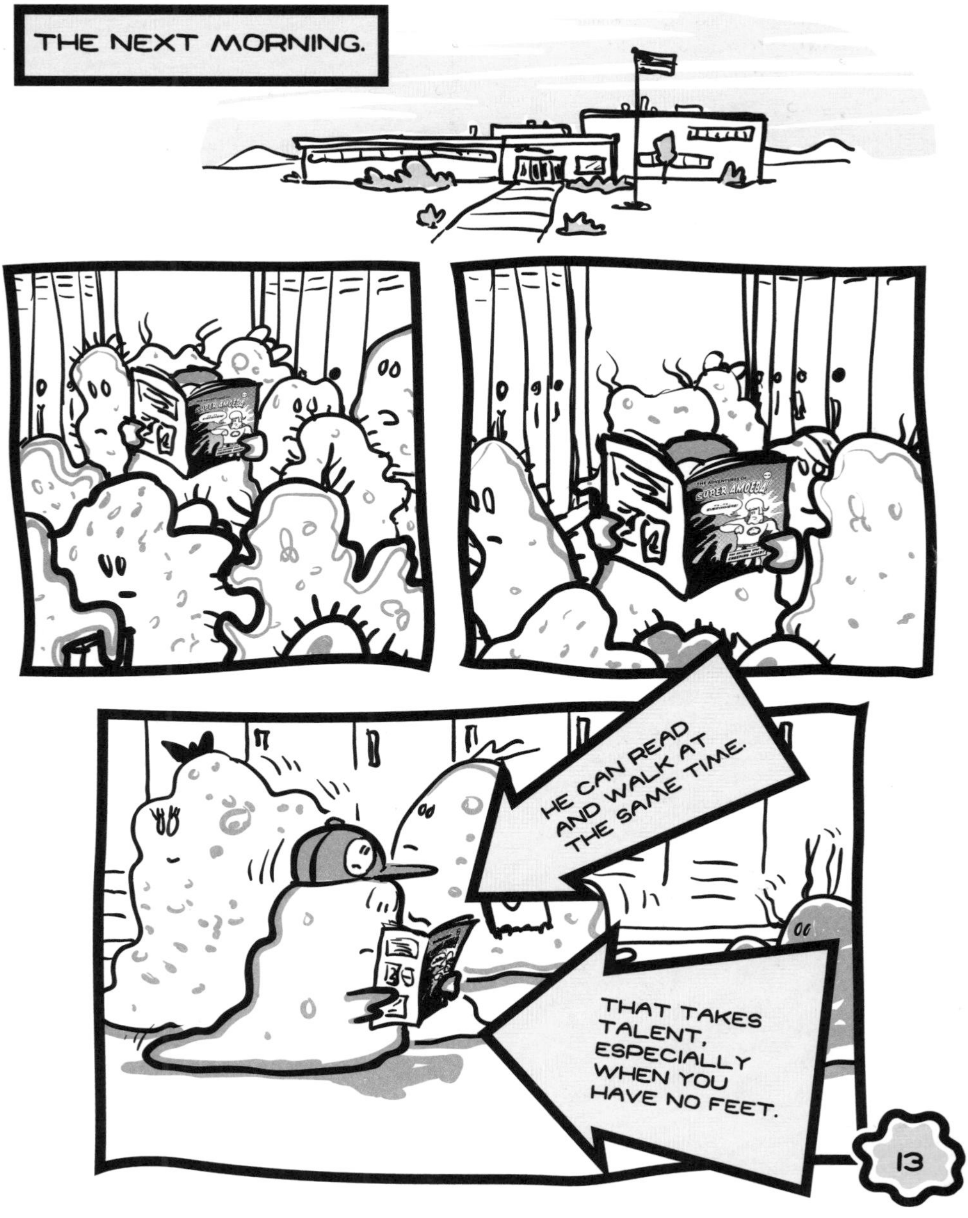
THE NEXT MORNING.
HE CAN READ AND WALK AT THE SAME TIME.
THAT TAKES TALENT, ESPECIALLY WHEN YOU HAVE NO FEET.

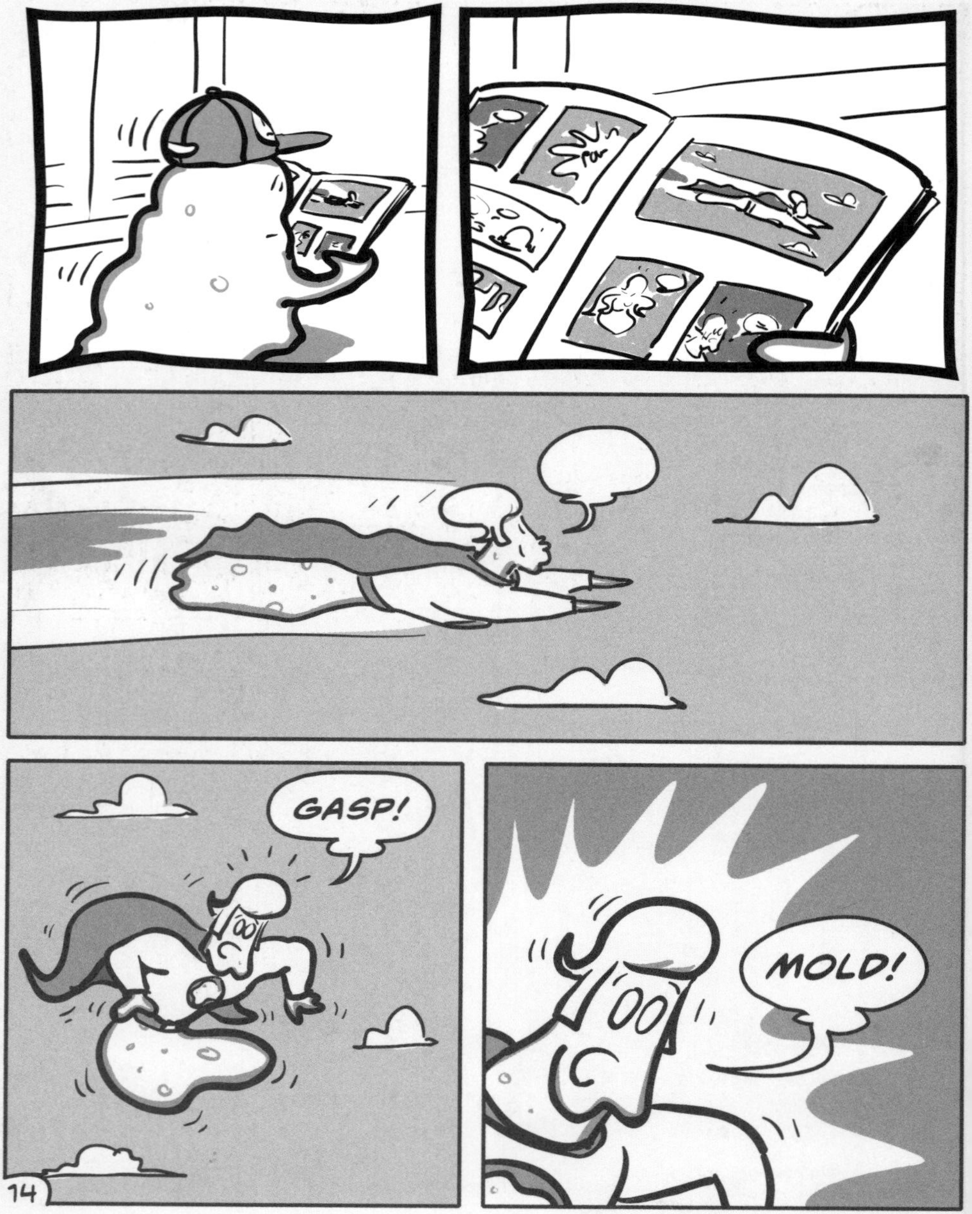
GASP!
MOLD!

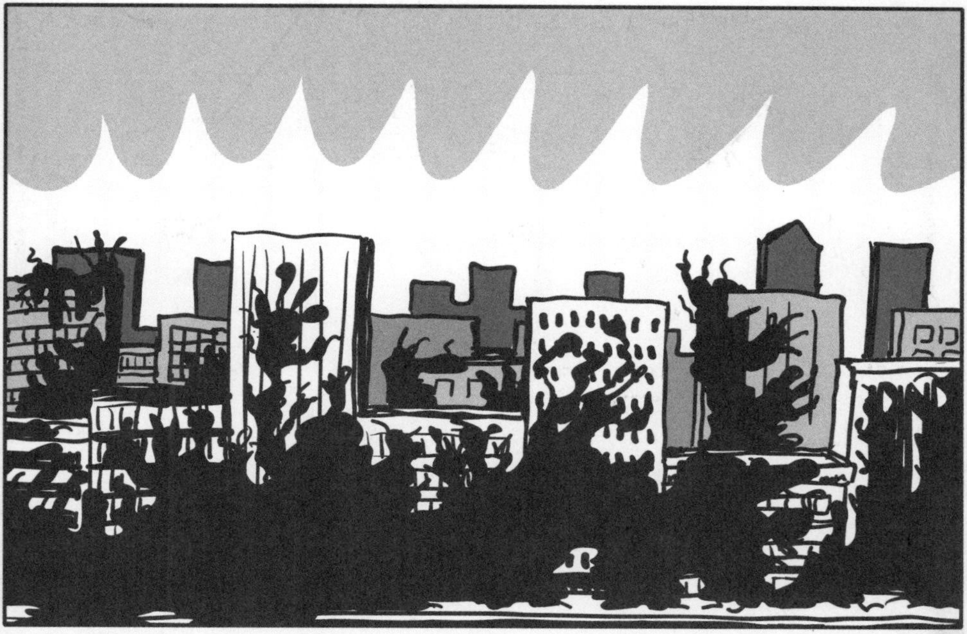

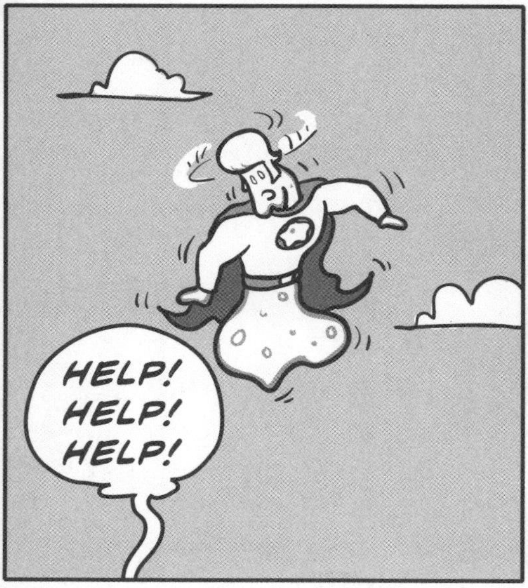
HELP! HELP! HELP!

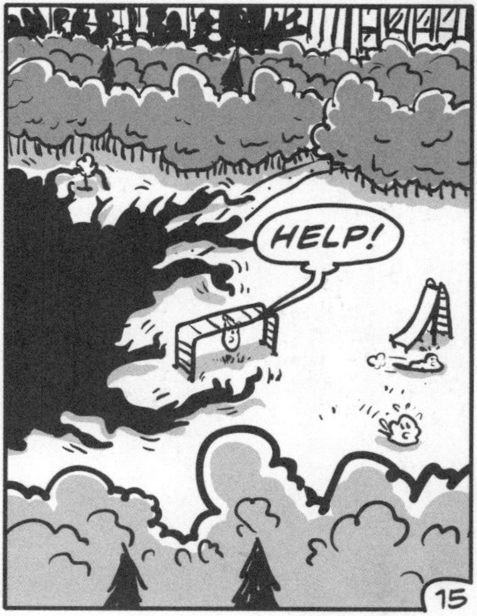
HELP!

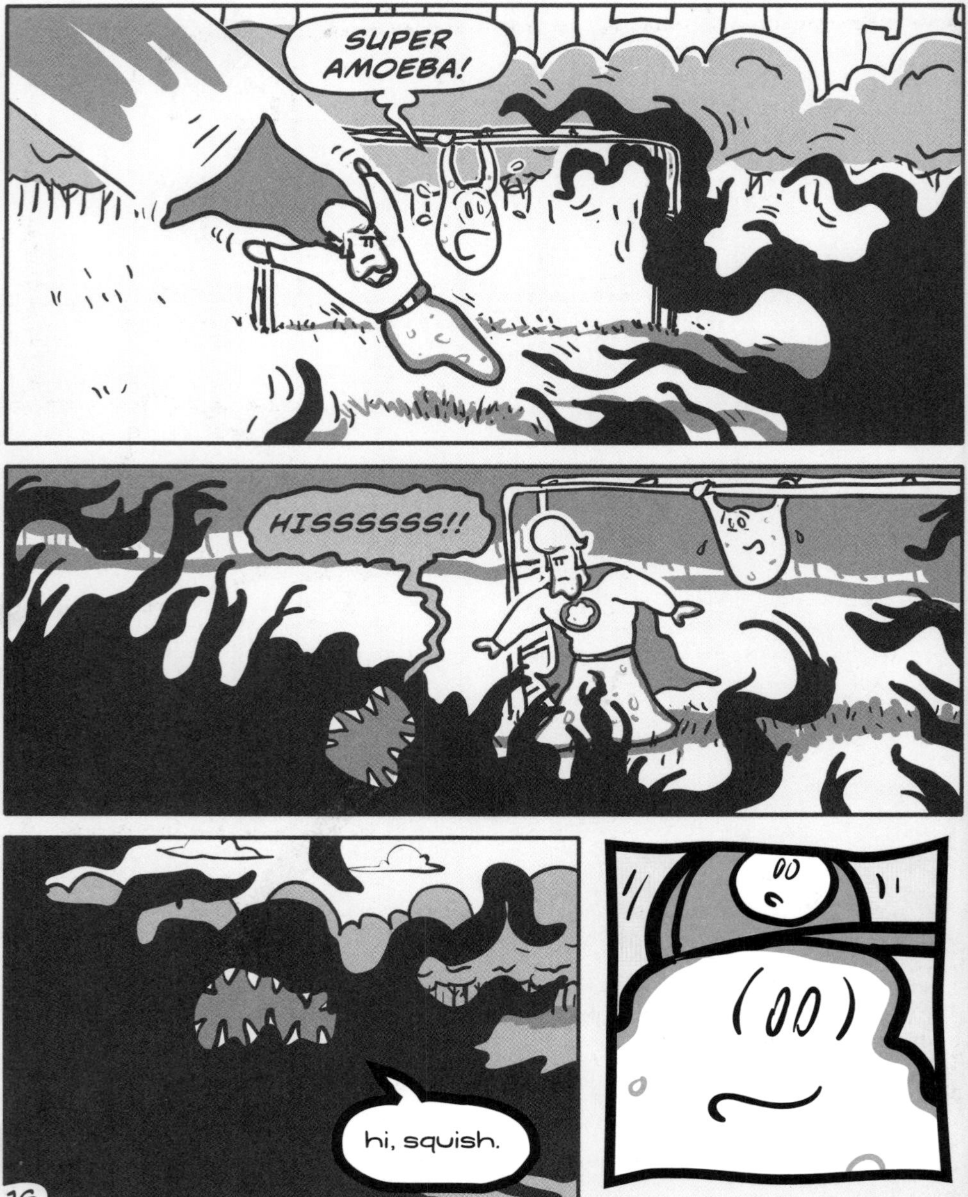
SUPER AMOEBA!
HISSSSSS!!
hi, squish.

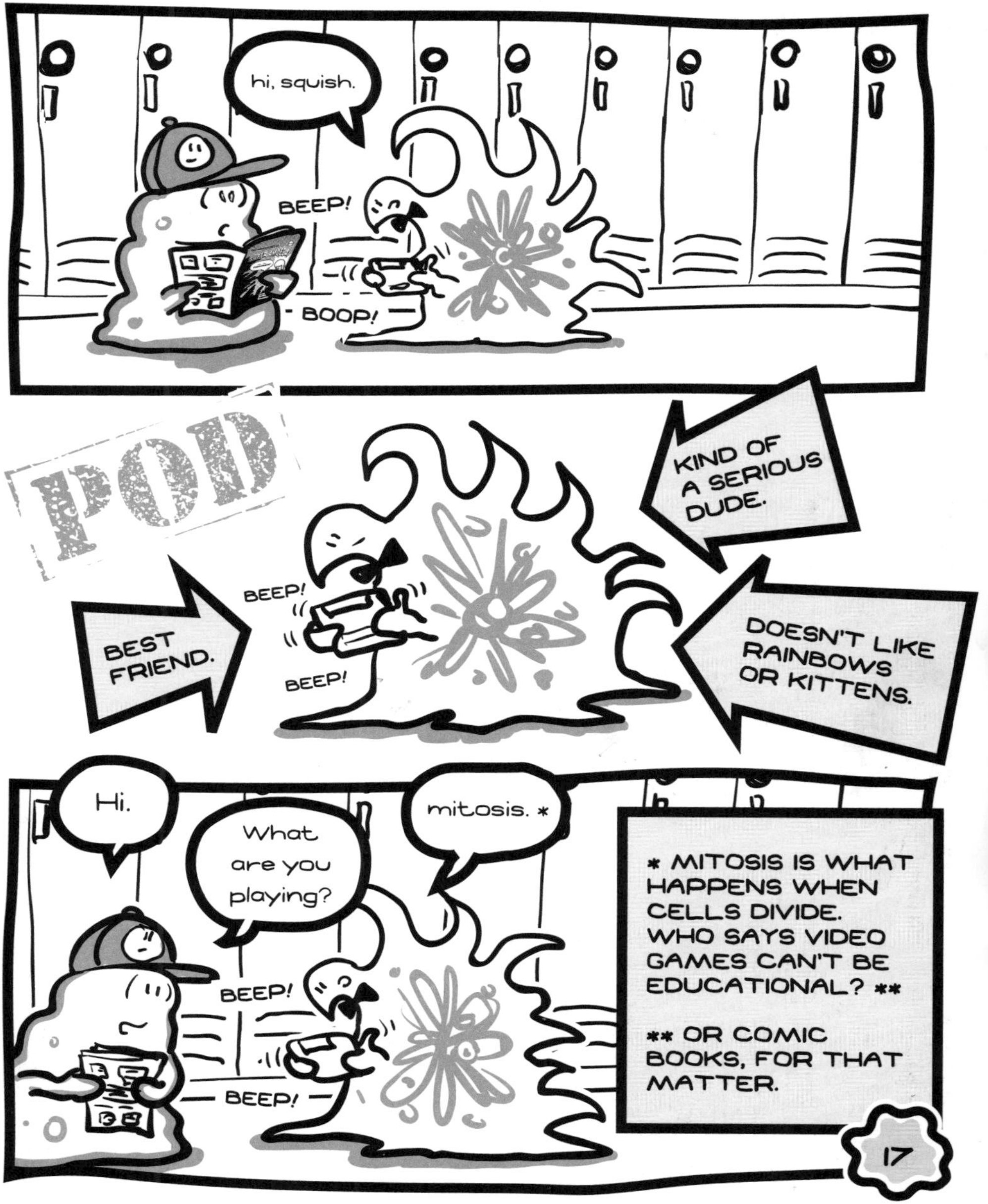
hi, squish.
BEEP!
BOOP!
POD
BEST FRIEND.
KIND OF A SERIOUS DUDE.
DOESN'T LIKE RAINBOWS OR KITTENS.
BEEP!
BEEP!
Hi.
What are you playing?
mitosis. *
BEEP!
BEEP!
* MITOSIS IS WHAT HAPPENS WHEN CELLS DIVIDE. WHO SAYS VIDEO GAMES CAN'T BE EDUCATIONAL? **
** OR COMIC BOOKS, FOR THAT MATTER.

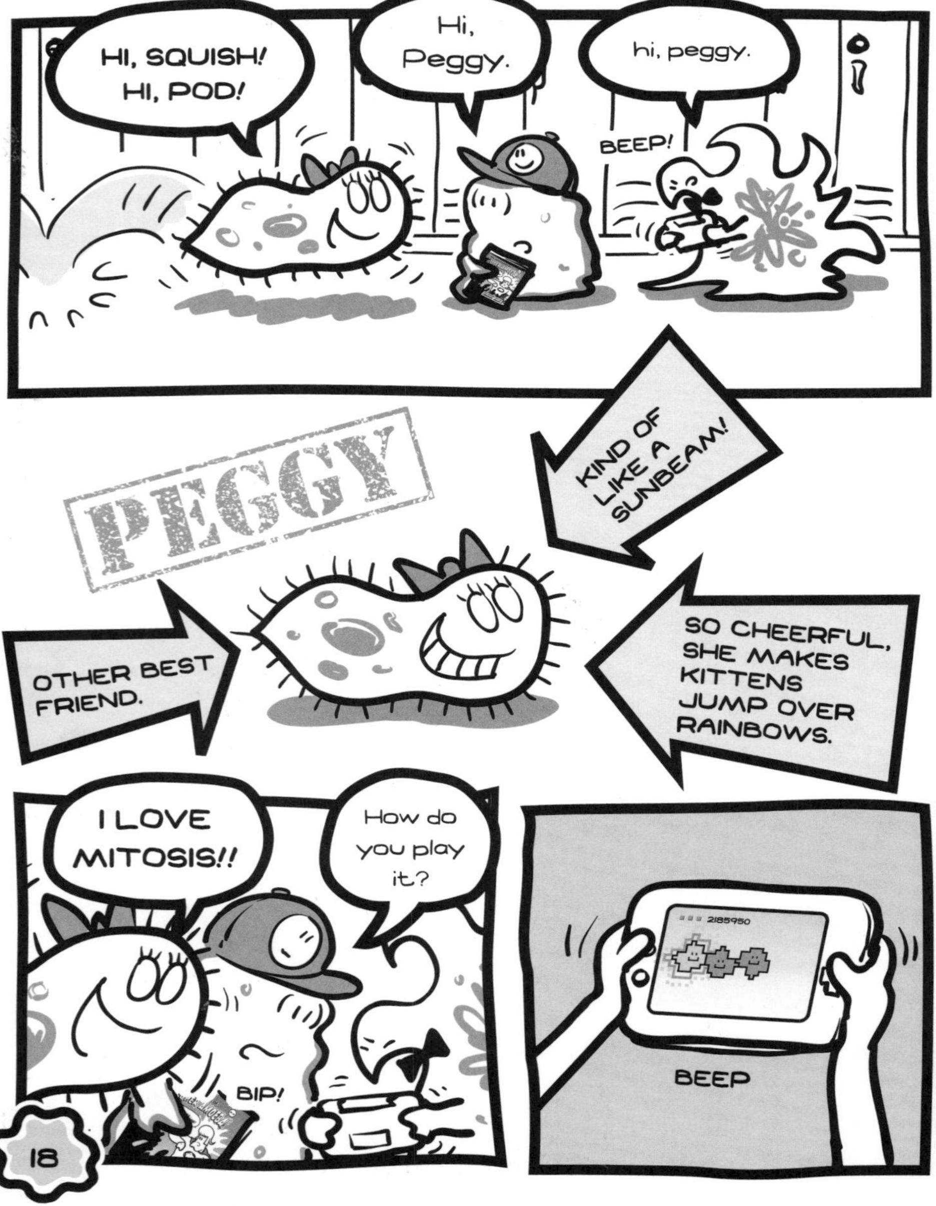
HI, SQUISH!
HI, POD!
Hi,
Peggy.
hi, peggy.
BEEP!
PEGGY
OTHER BEST FRIEND.
KIND OF LIKE A SUNBEAM!
SO CHEERFUL, SHE MAKES KITTENS JUMP OVER RAINBOWS.
I LOVE MITOSIS!!
How do you play it?
BIP!
2185950
BEEP

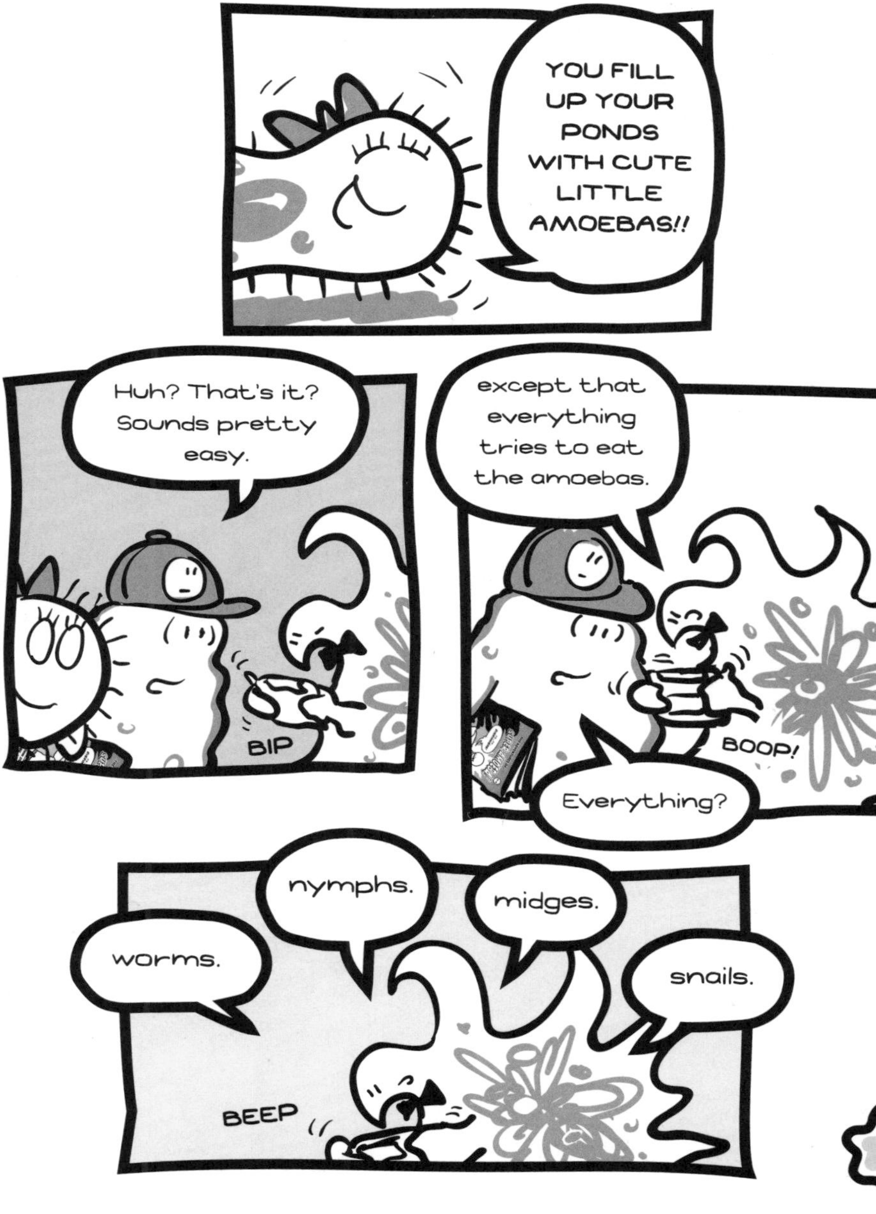
YOU FILL UP YOUR PONDS WITH CUTE LITTLE AMOEBAS!!
Huh? That's it? Sounds pretty easy.
BIP
except that everything tries to eat the amoebas.
BOOP!
Everything?
worms.
nymphs.
midges.
snails.
BEEP

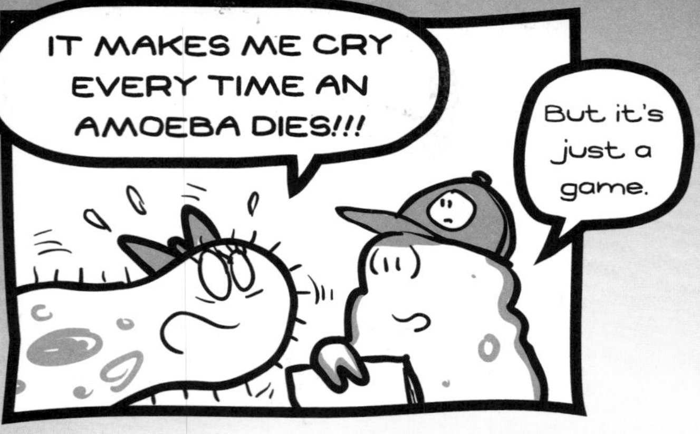
IT MAKES ME CRY EVERY TIME AN AMOEBA DIES!!!
But it's just a game.

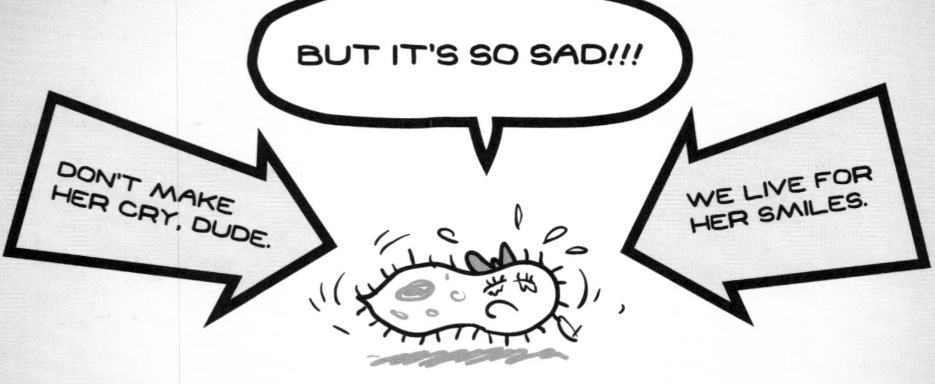
BUT IT'S SO SAD!!!
DON'T MAKE HER CRY, DUDE.
WE LIVE FOR HER SMILES.

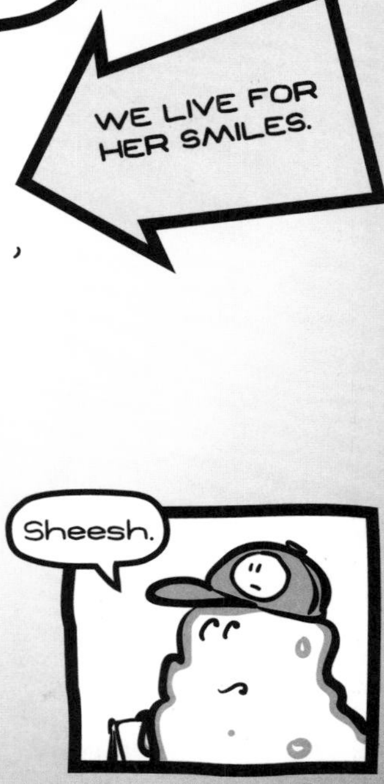
Sheesh.

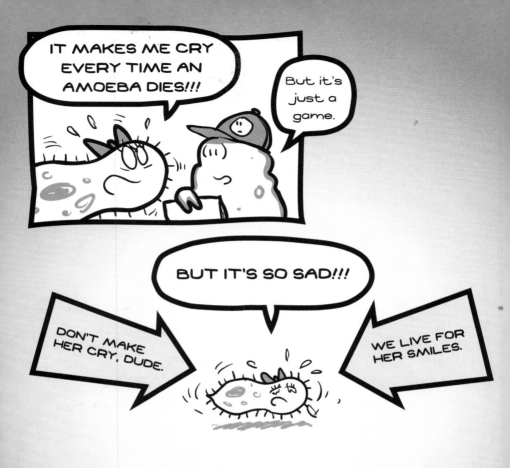

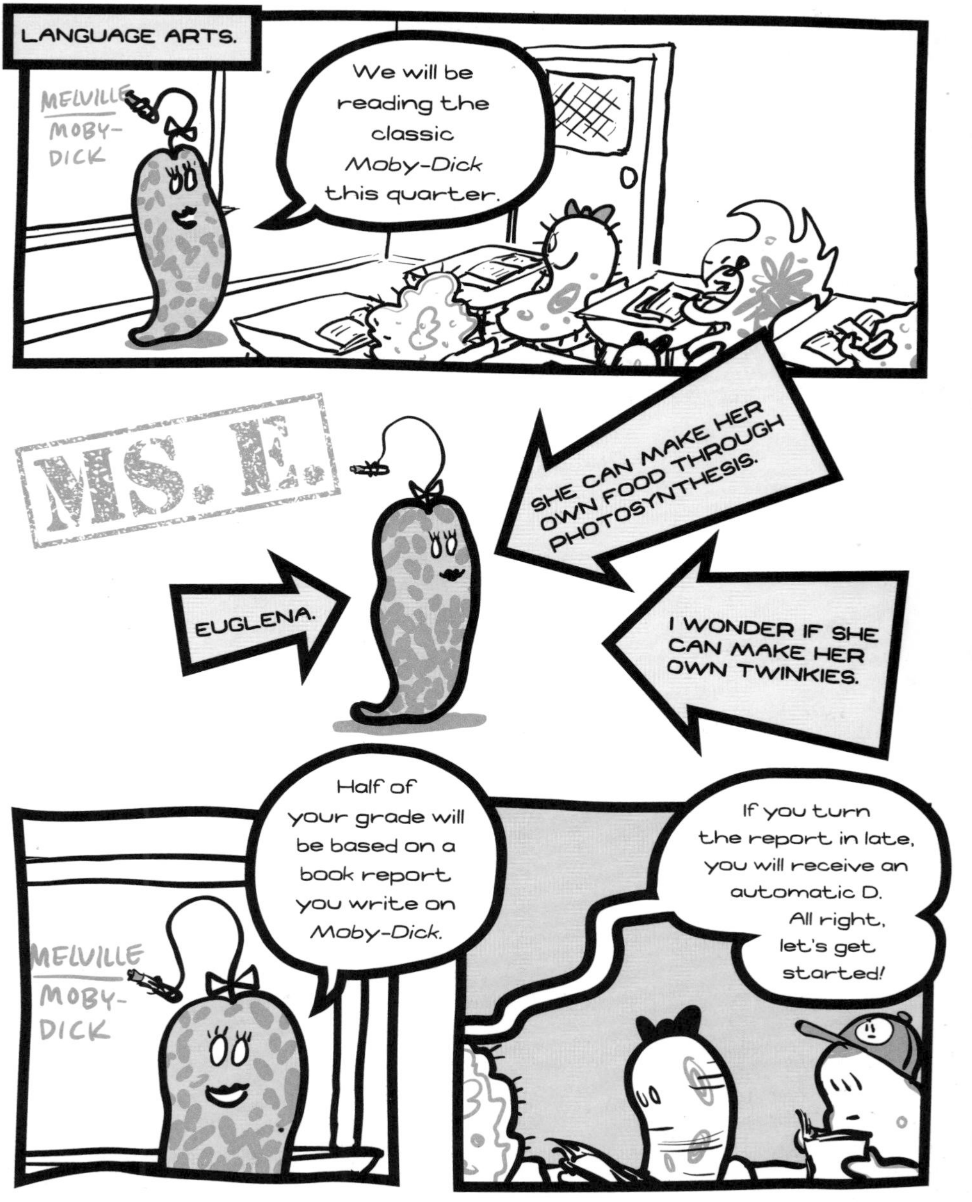

LANGUAGE ARTS.
MELVILLE
MOBY-DICK
We will be reading the classic *Moby-Dick* this quarter.
MS. E.
SHE CAN MAKE HER OWN FOOD THROUGH PHOTOSYNTHESIS.
EUGLENA.
I WONDER IF SHE CAN MAKE HER OWN TWINKIES.
MELVILLE
MOBY-DICK
Half of your grade will be based on a book report you write on *Moby-Dick*.
If you turn the report in late, you will receive an automatic D. All right, let's get started!

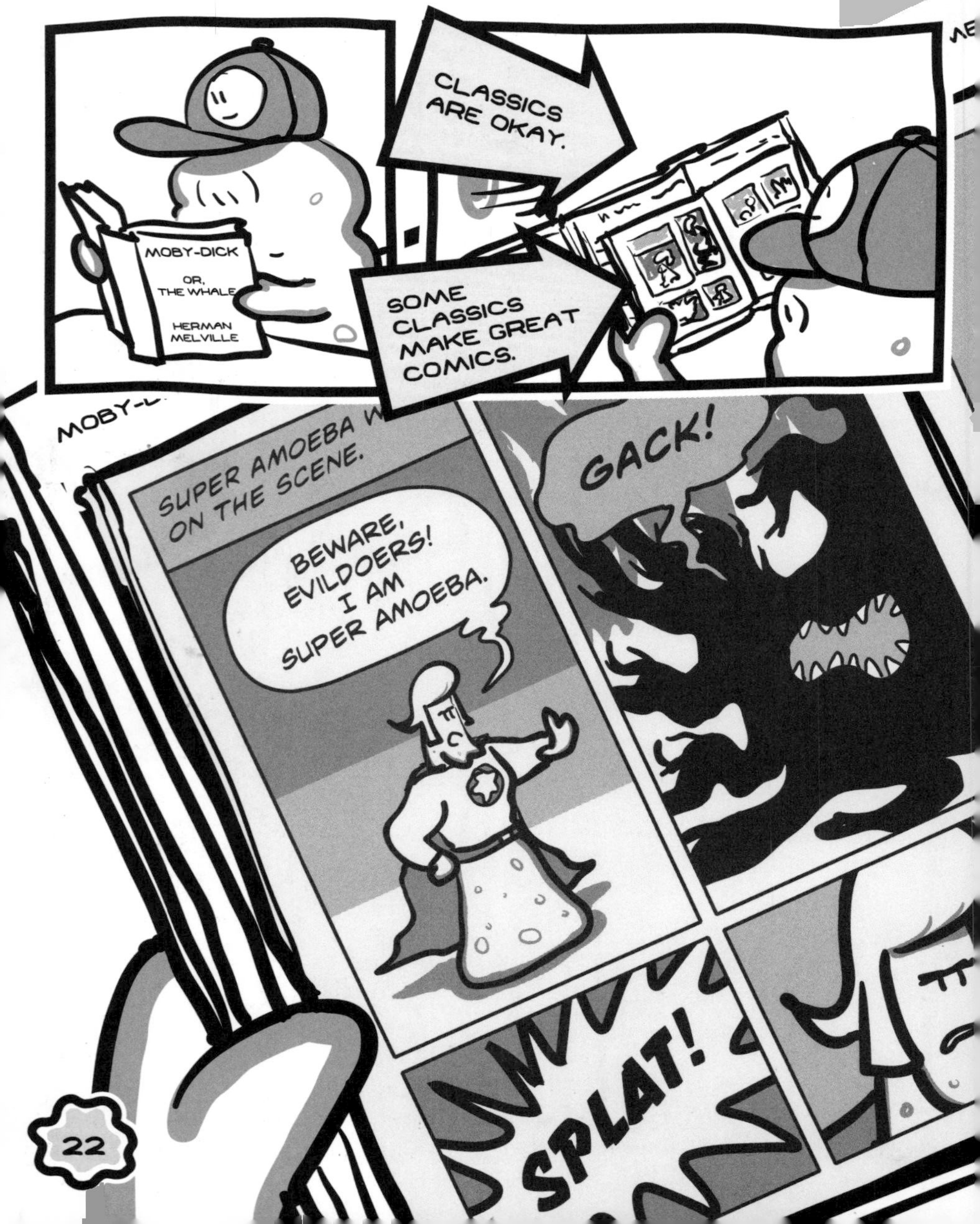
MOBY-DICK
OR, THE WHALE
HERMAN MELVILLE
CLASSICS ARE OKAY.
SOME CLASSICS MAKE GREAT COMICS.
SUPER AMOEBA W
ON THE SCENE.
BEWARE, EVILDOERS! I AM SUPER AMOEBA.
GACK!
SPLAT!

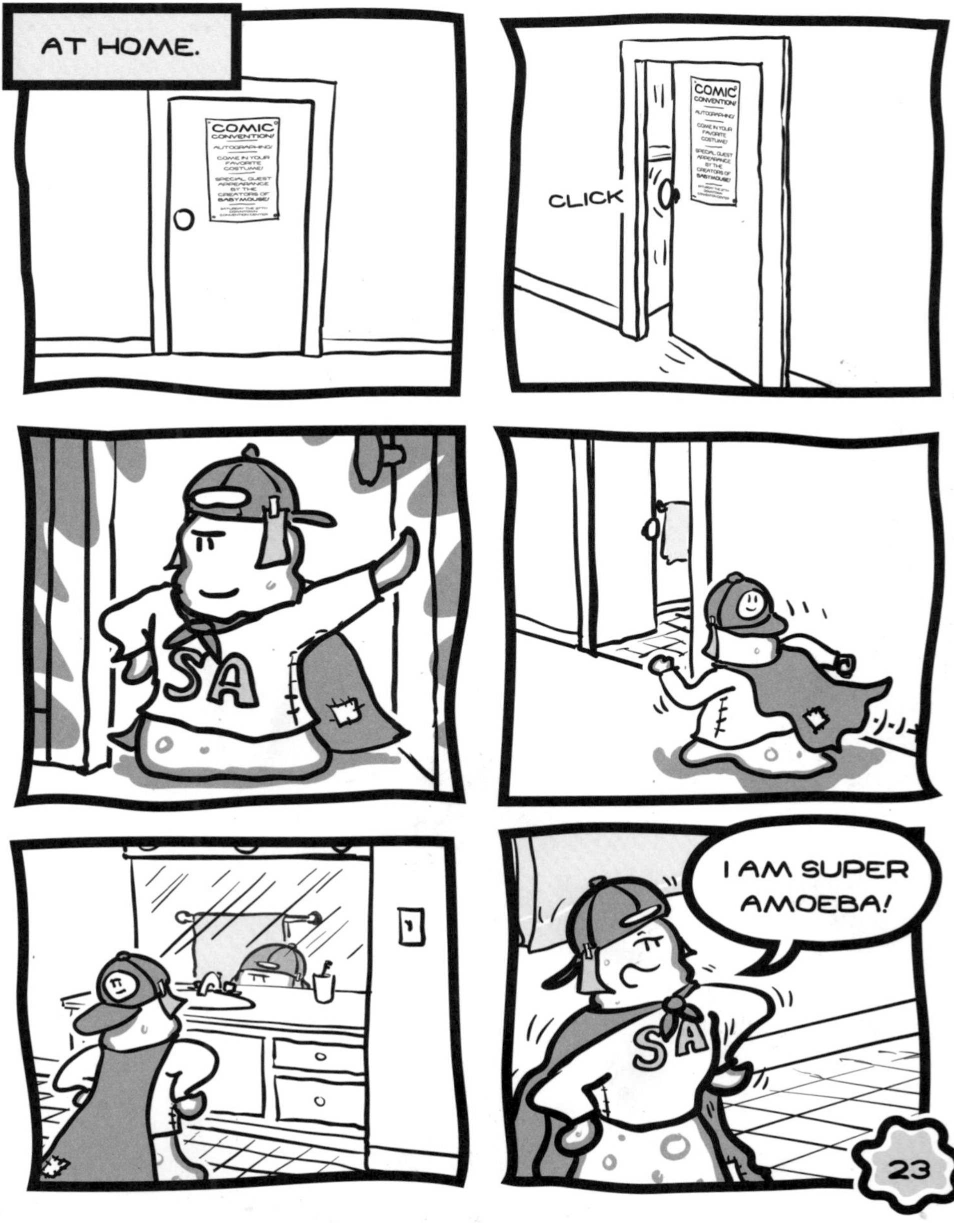
AT HOME.
COMIC CONVENTION!
AUTOGRAPHING!
COME IN YOUR FAVORITE COSTUME!
SPECIAL GUEST APPEARANCE BY THE CREATORS OF BABYMOUSE!
CLICK
I AM SUPER AMOEBA!

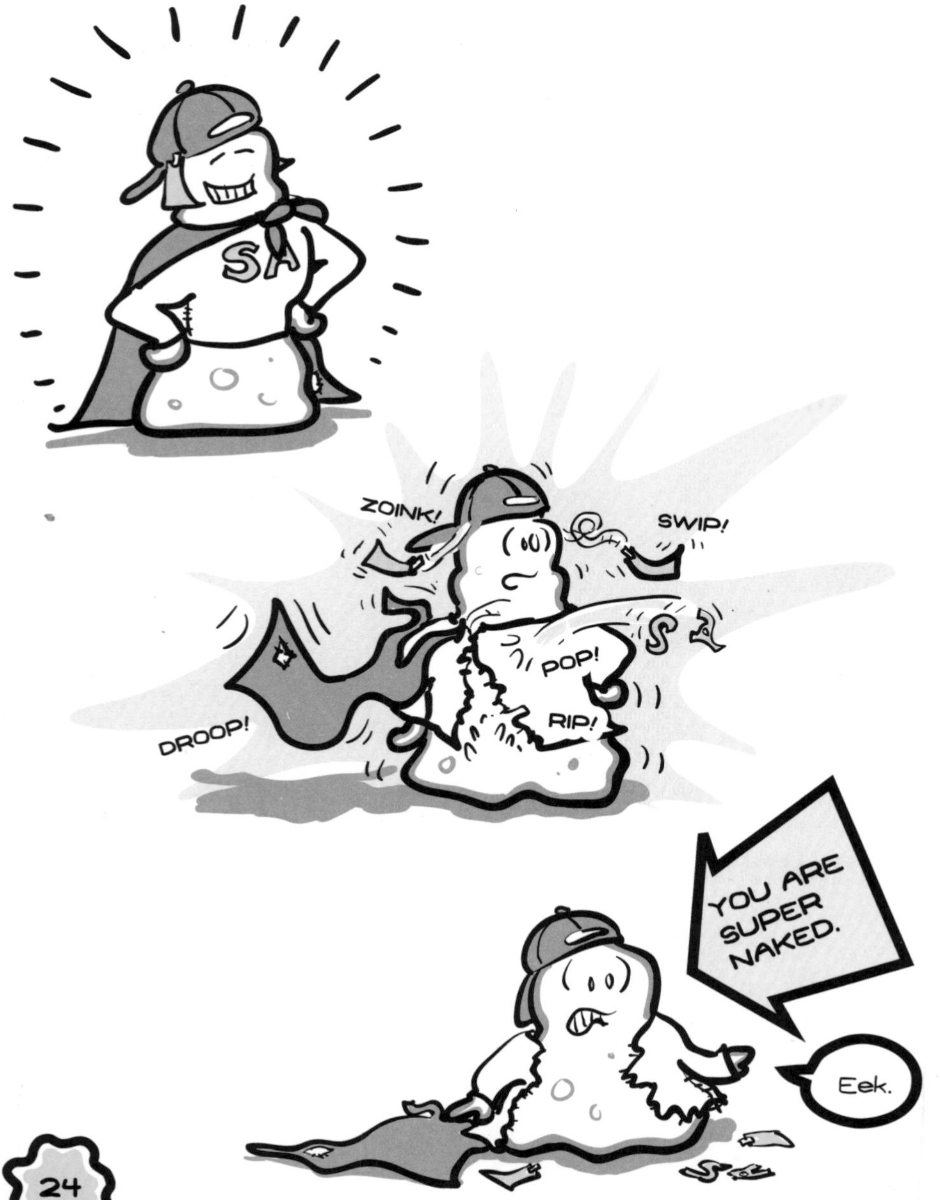
ZOINK!
SWIP!
POP!
RIP!
DROOP!
YOU ARE SUPER NAKED.
Eek.

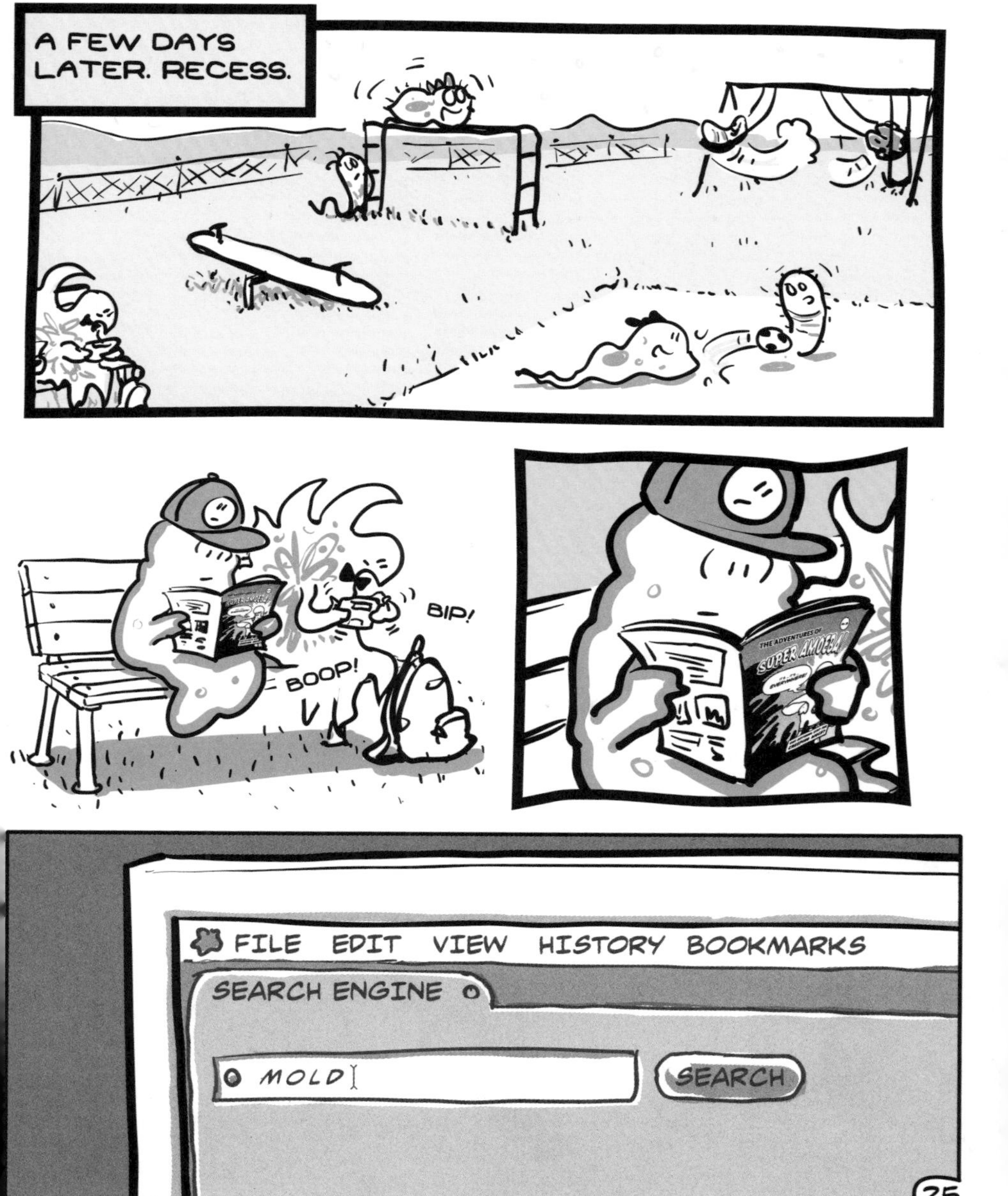
A FEW DAYS LATER. RECESS.
BIP!
BOOP!
THE ADVENTURES OF
SUPER AMOEBA!
FILE EDIT VIEW HISTORY BOOKMARKS
SEARCH ENGINE
MOLD
SEARCH

SEARCH RESULTS

- *KILL MOLD WITH BLEACH.* YOU CAN ELIMINATE MOST MOLDS AND MILDEWS WITH A DILUTED SOLUTI OF HOUSEHOLD BLEACH *(SODIUM HYPOCHLORITE)* . . .

- *MOLDY CHEESES.* THE MAJORITY OF THE WORLD'S MOST NOTABLE RIPENED CHEESES TRACE THEIR ORI TO ANCIENT TIMES. ROQUEFORT IS FIRST . . .

- *FUNGI AND MOLDS BY SPECIES.* THE CLASSIFIC AND STUDY OF MOLDS AND FUNGI (FUNGUSES) IS KNO

LEAN

SIGH.

I'M GOING TO NEED A LOT OF BLEACH.

RUB RUB

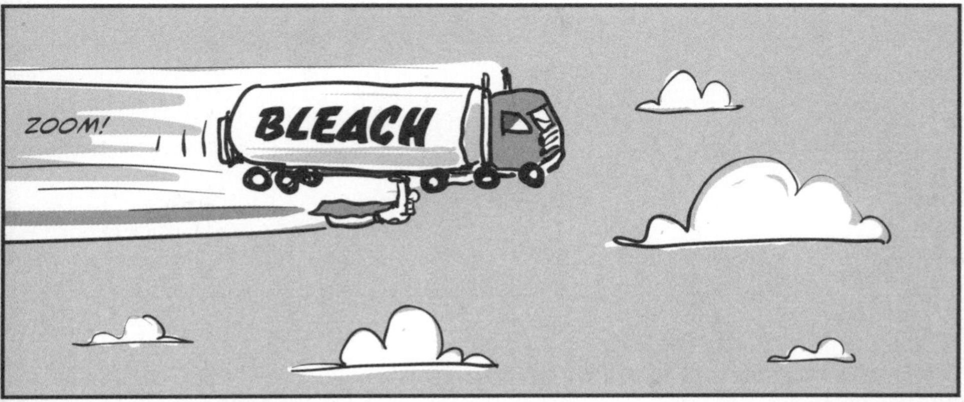
ZOOM!
BLEACH

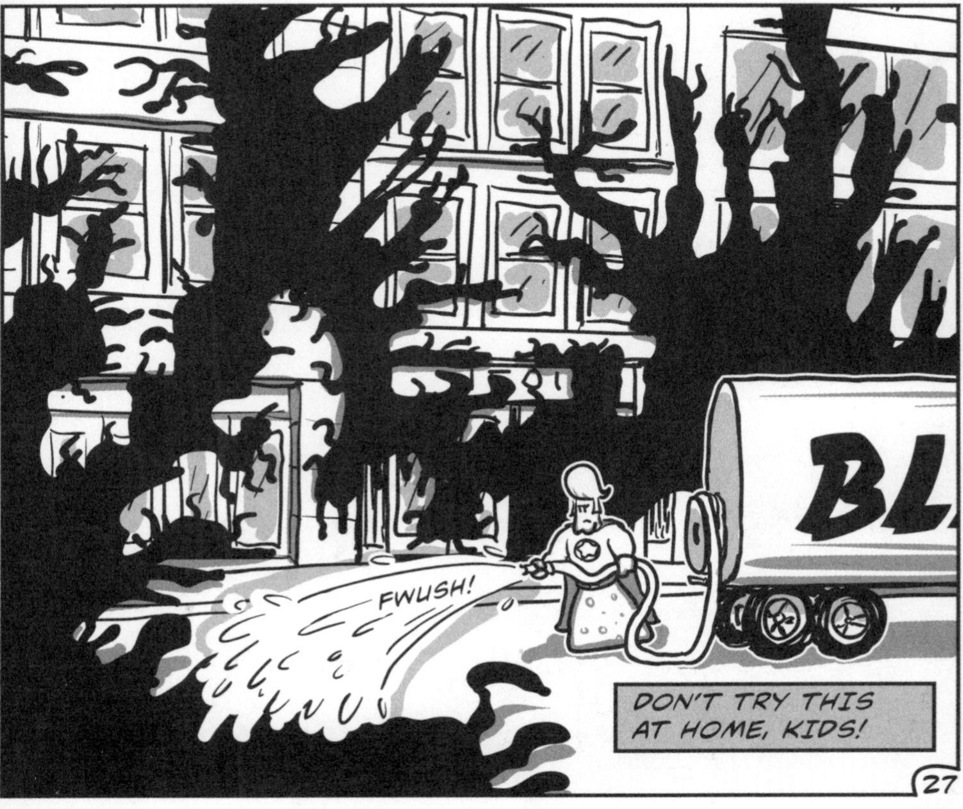
BL
FWUSH!
DON'T TRY THIS AT HOME, KIDS!

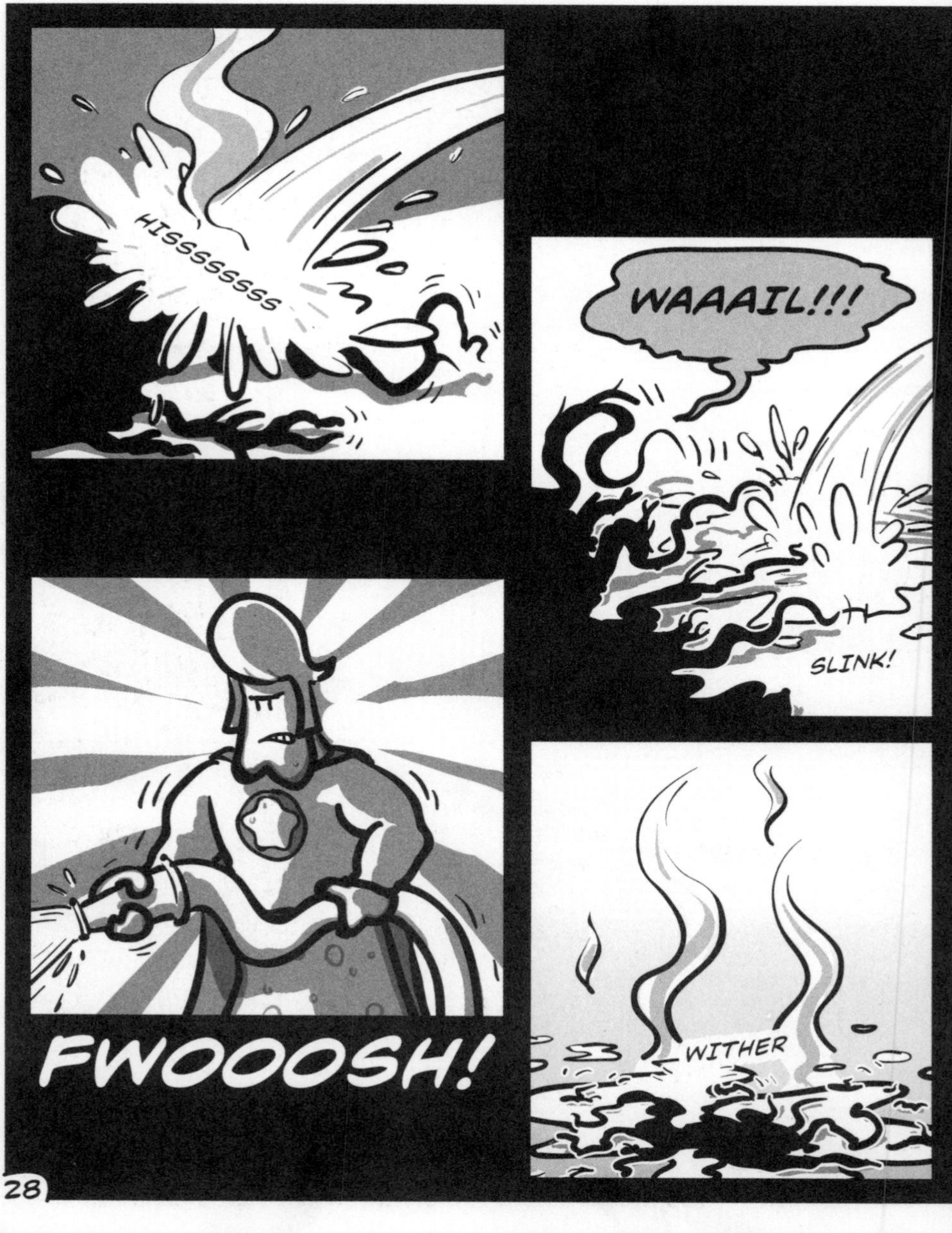
HISSSSSSSSS
WAAAIL!!!
SLINK!
FWOOOSH!
WITHER

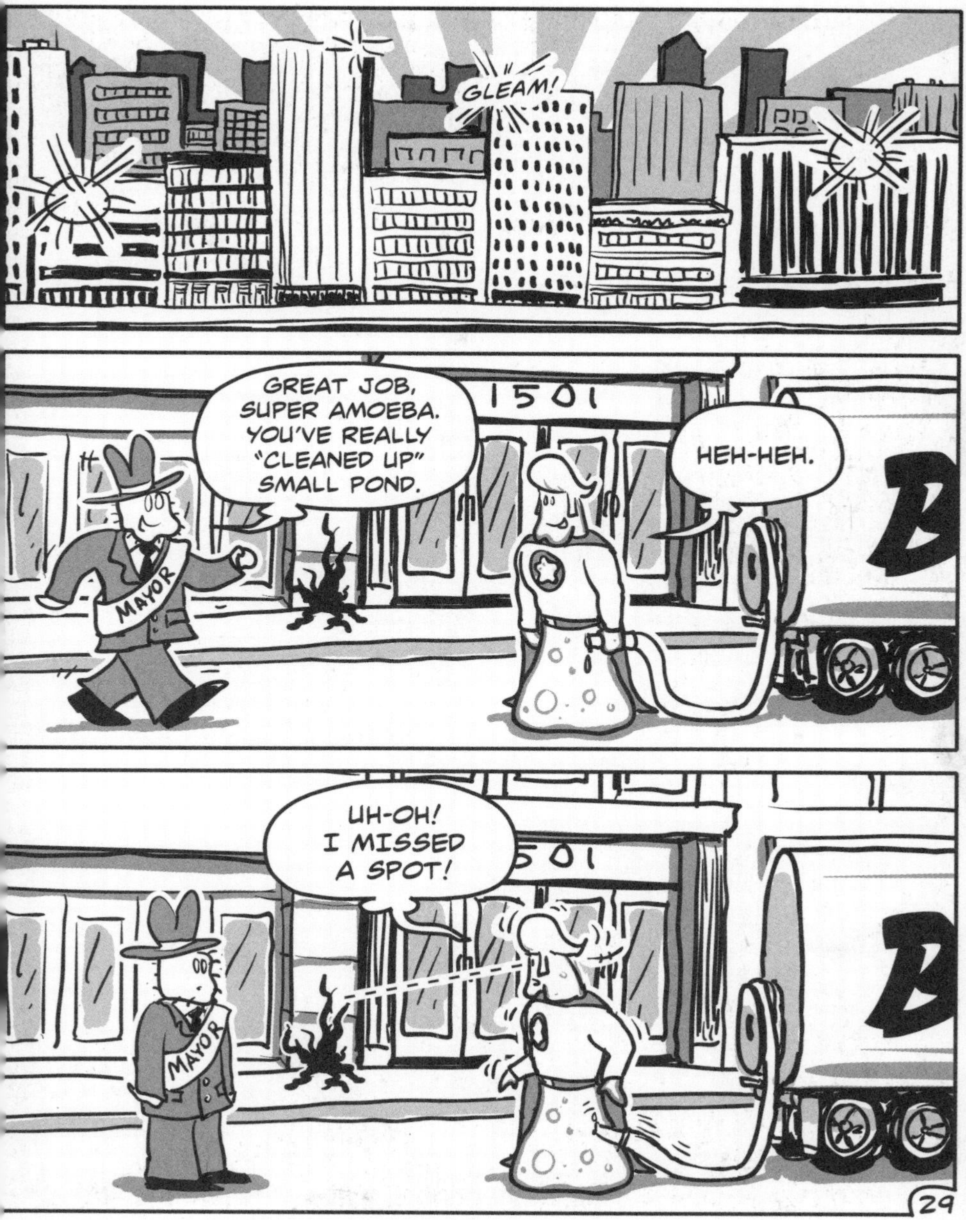
GLEAM!
1501
GREAT JOB, SUPER AMOEBA. YOU'VE REALLY "CLEANED UP" SMALL POND.
HEH-HEH.
MAYOR
UH-OH! I MISSED A SPOT!
MAYOR

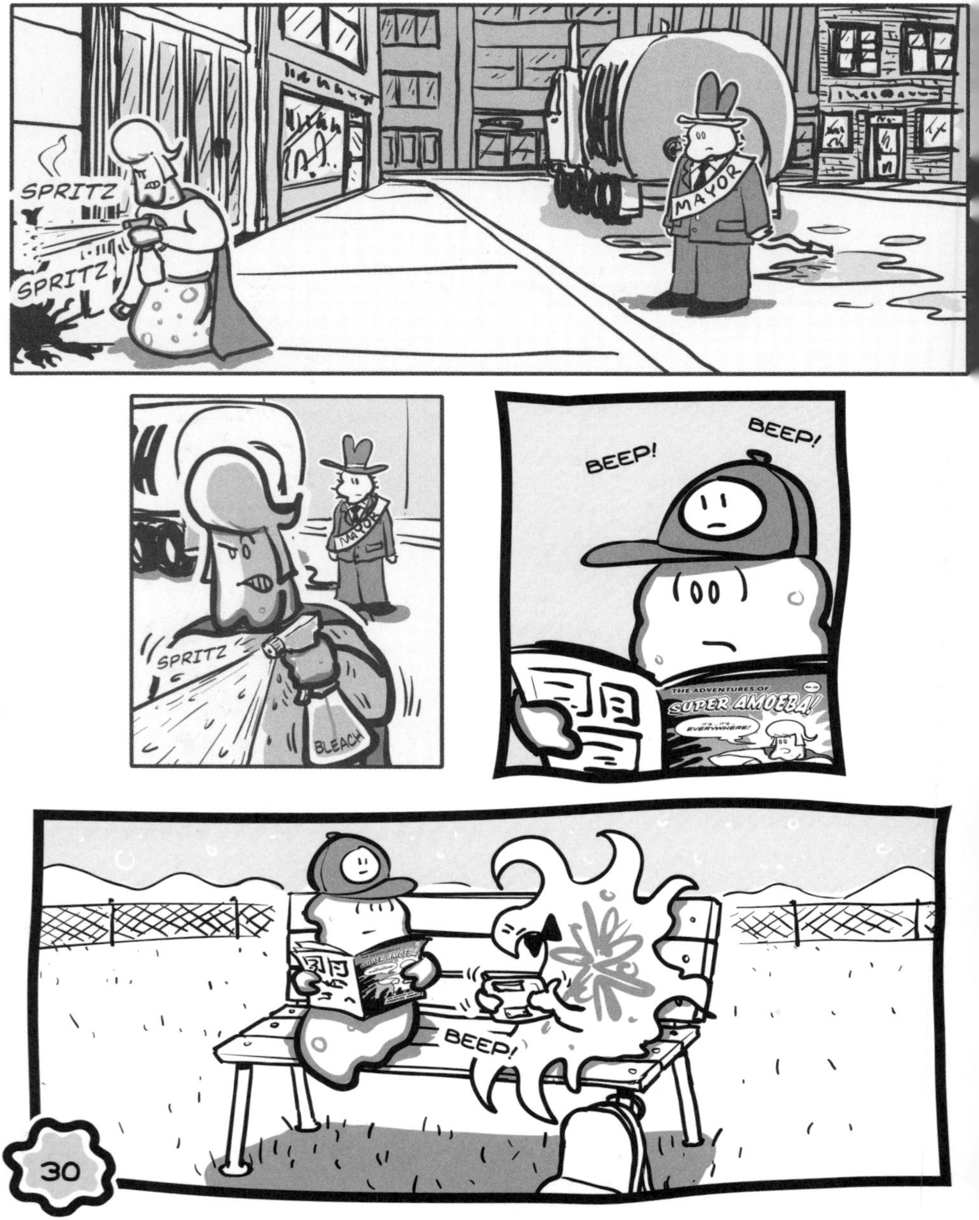
SPRITZ
SPRITZ
MAYOR
SPRITZ
MAYOR
BLEACH
BEEP!
BEEP!
THE ADVENTURES OF
SUPER AMOEBA!
IT'S... IT'S... EVERYWHERE!
BEEP!

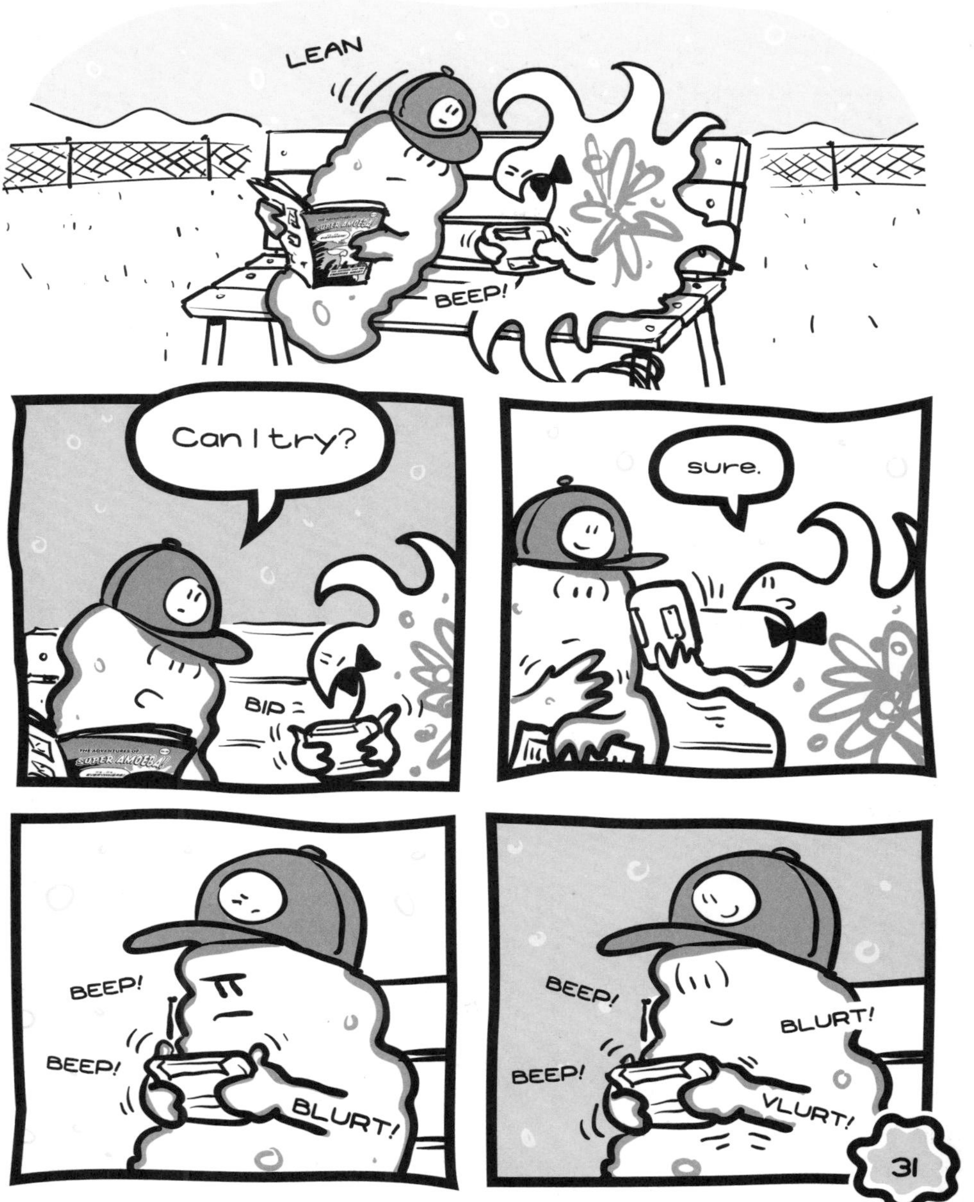
LEAN
BEEP!
Can I try?
SUPER AMOEBA!
BIP
sure.
BEEP!
BEEP!
BLURT!
BEEP!
BEEP!
BLURT!
VLURT!

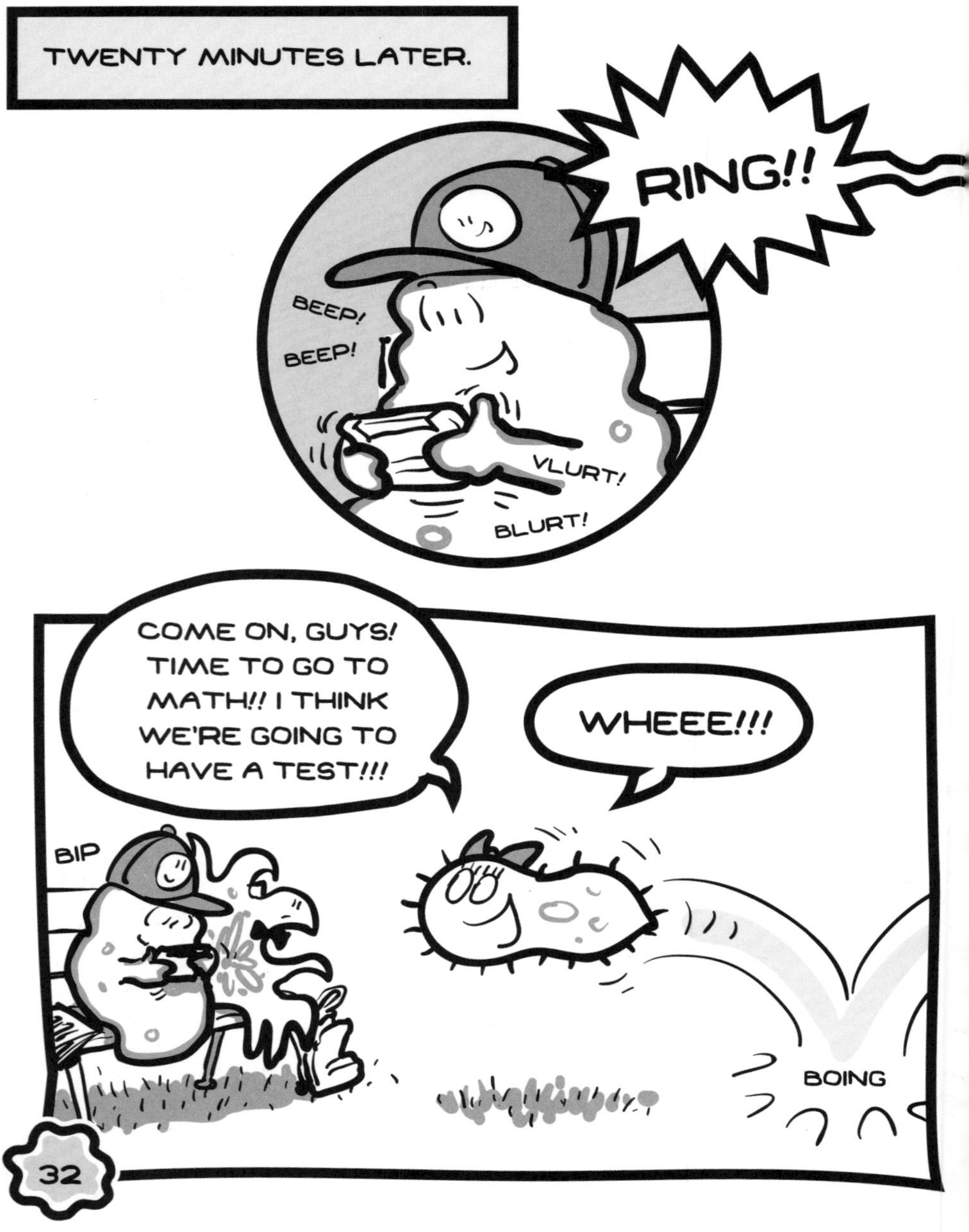
TWENTY MINUTES LATER.
RING!!
BEEP!
BEEP!
VLURT!
BLURT!
COME ON, GUYS! TIME TO GO TO MATH!! I THINK WE'RE GOING TO HAVE A TEST!!!
WHEEE!!!
BIP
BOING

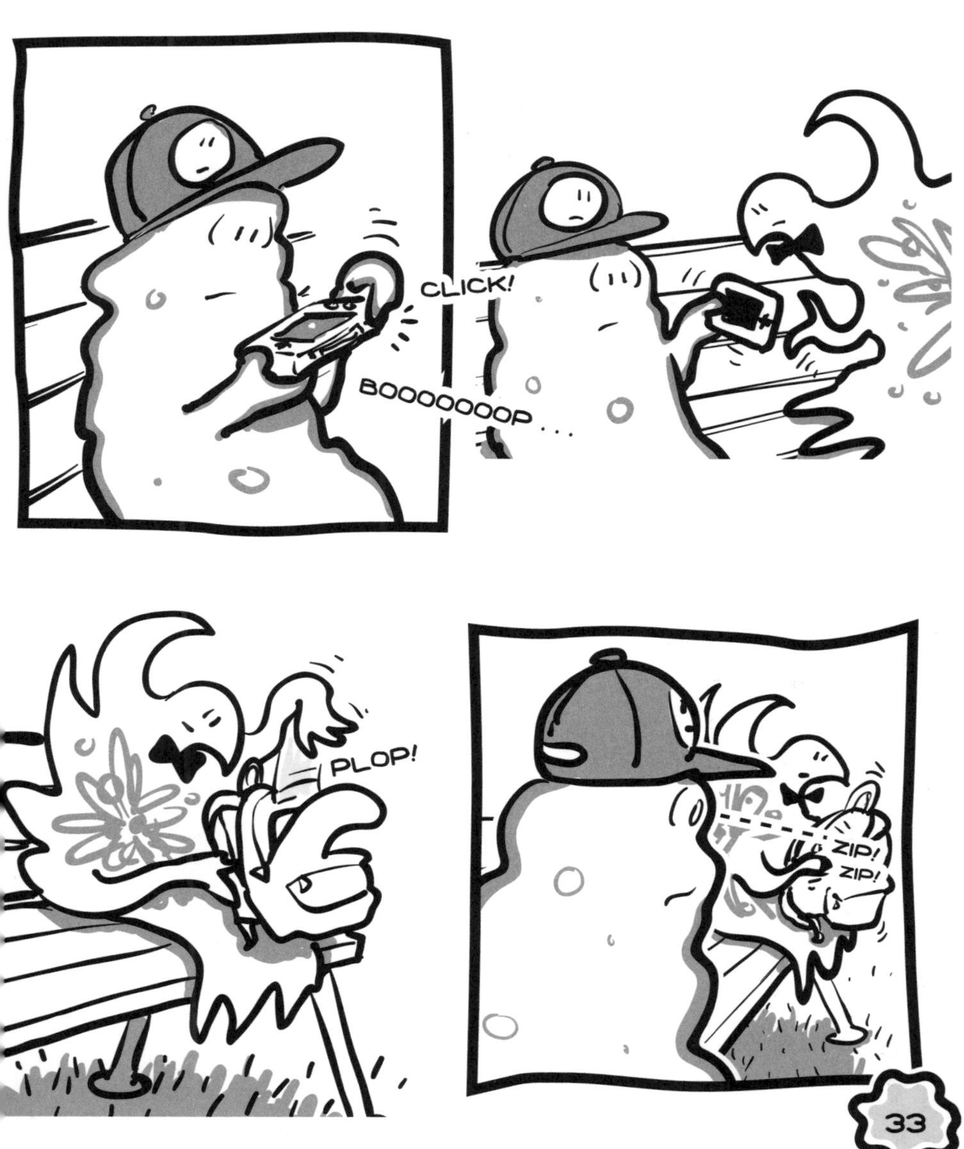
CLICK!
BOOOOOOOP...
PLOP!
ZIP!
ZIP!

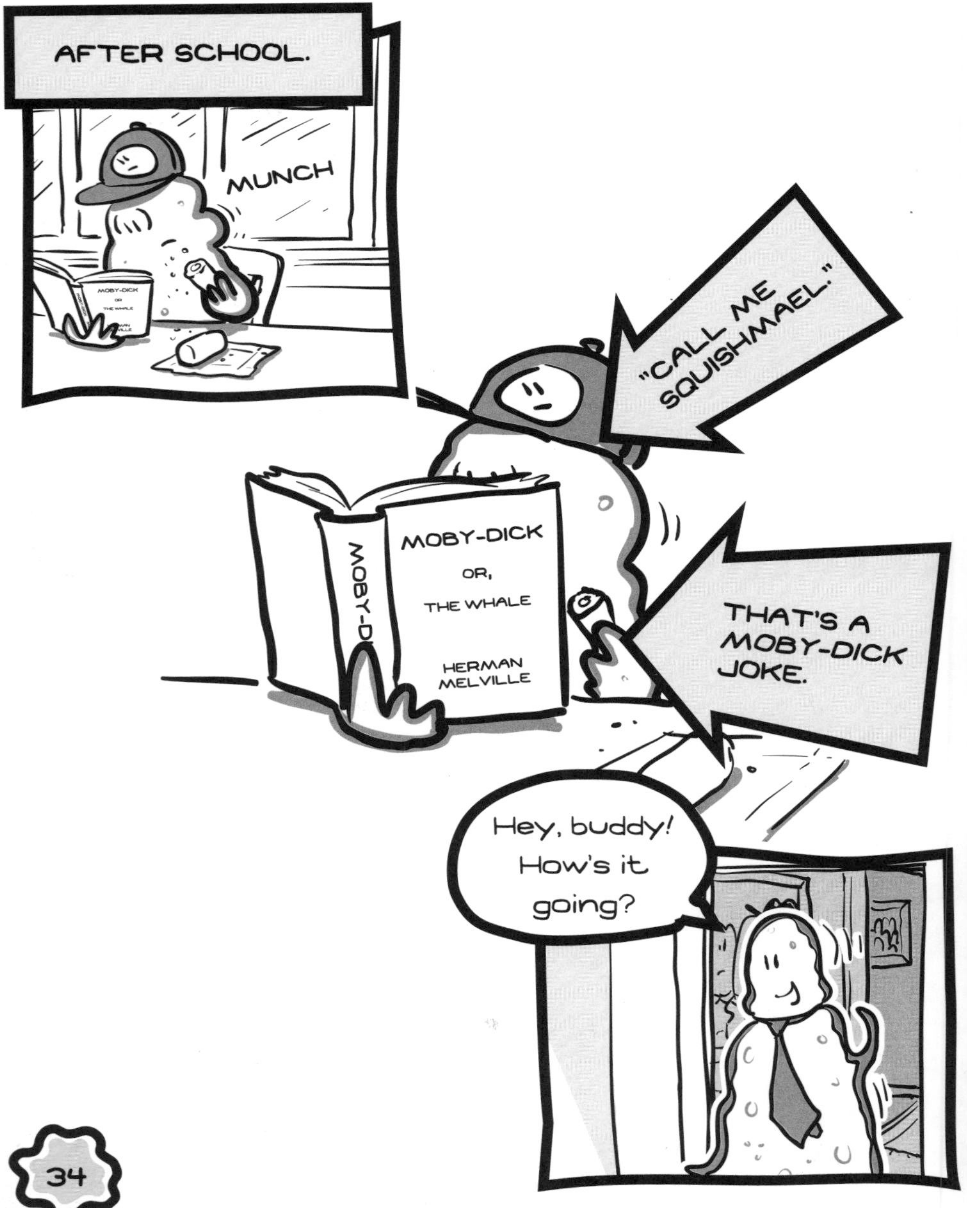
AFTER SCHOOL.
MUNCH
"CALL ME SQUISHMAEL."
MOBY-DICK OR, THE WHALE HERMAN MELVILLE
THAT'S A MOBY-DICK JOKE.
Hey, buddy! How's it going?

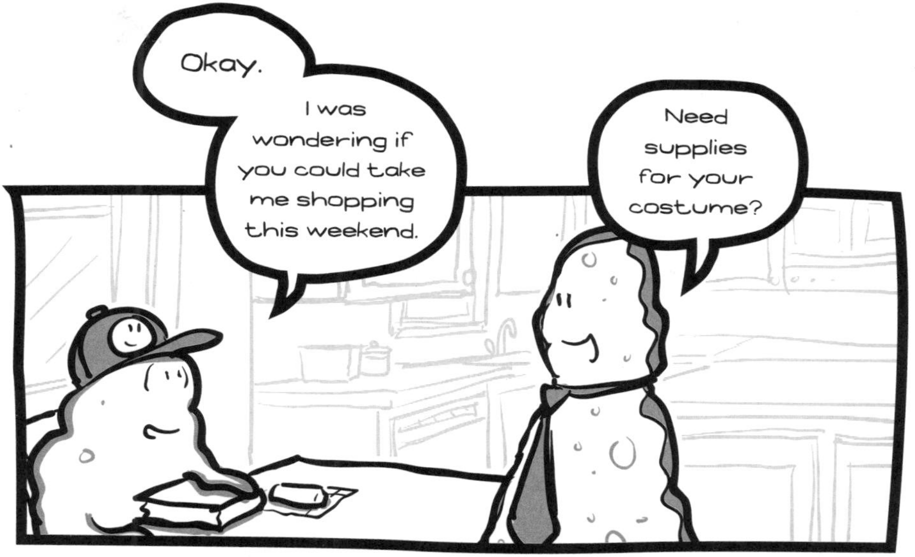
Okay.
I was wondering if you could take me shopping this weekend.
Need supplies for your costume?

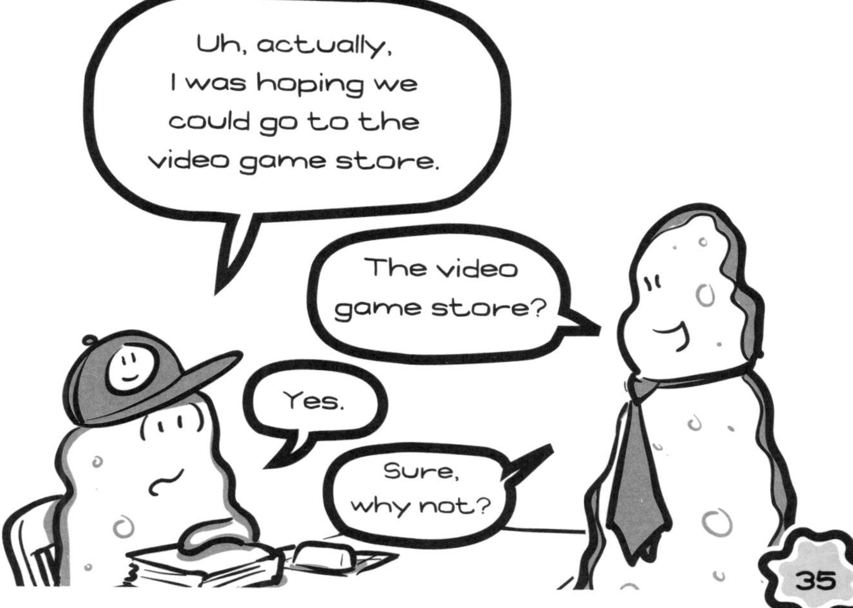
Uh, actually, I was hoping we could go to the video game store.
The video game store?
Yes.
Sure, why not?

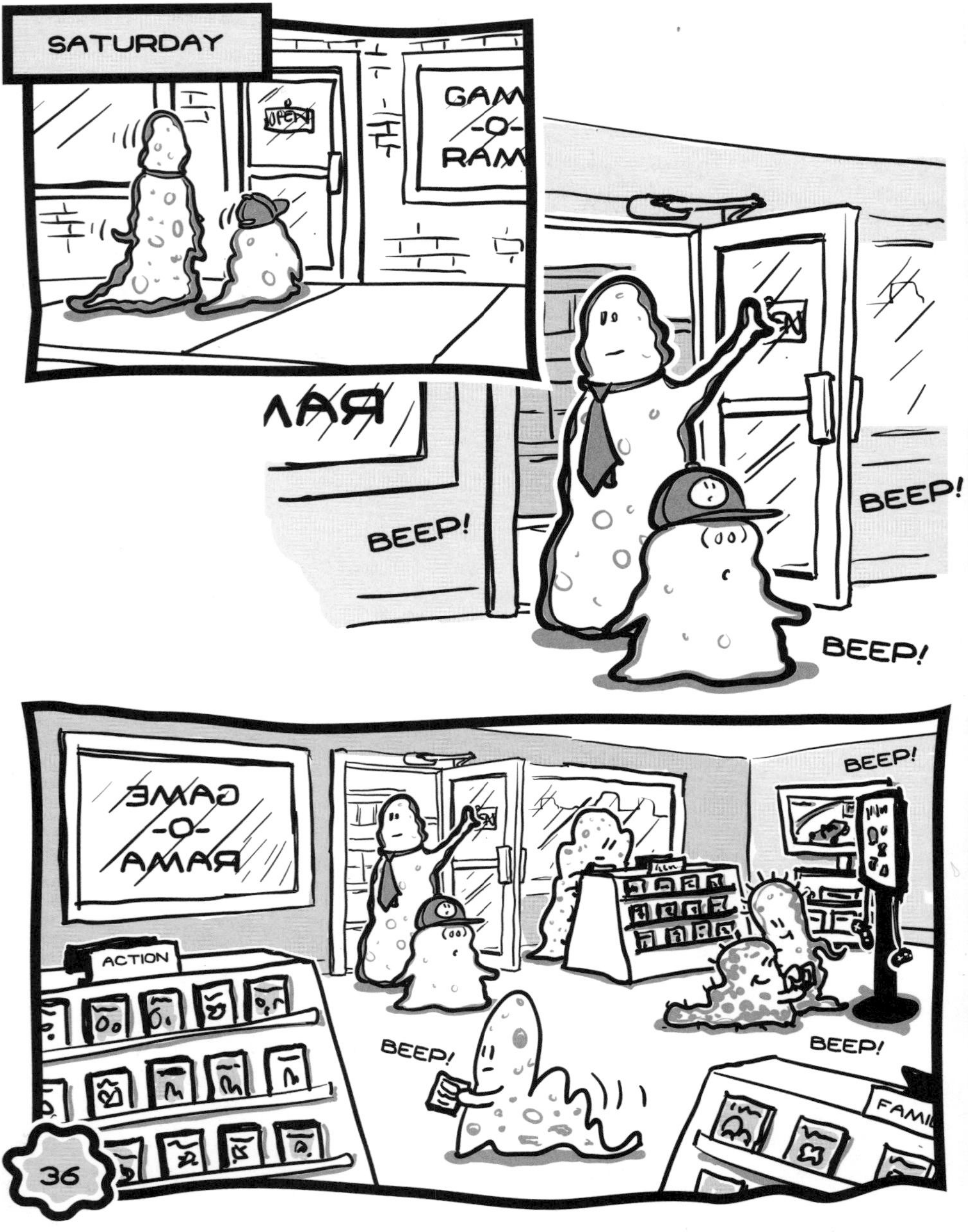
SATURDAY
GAM
-O-
RAM
BEEP!
BEEP!
BEEP!
ACTION
BEEP!
BEEP!
BEEP!

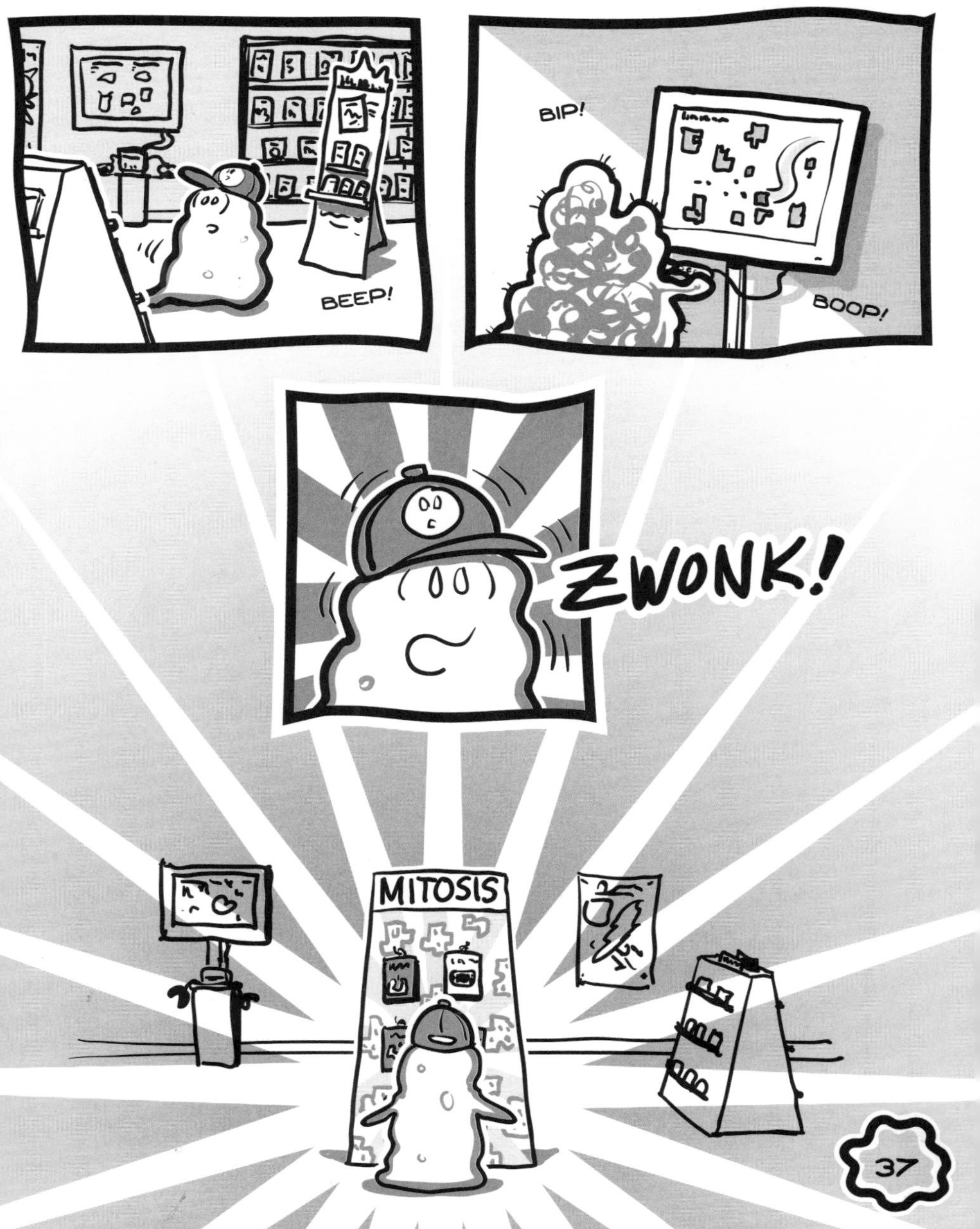
BEEP!
BIP!
BOOP!
ZWONK!
MITOSIS

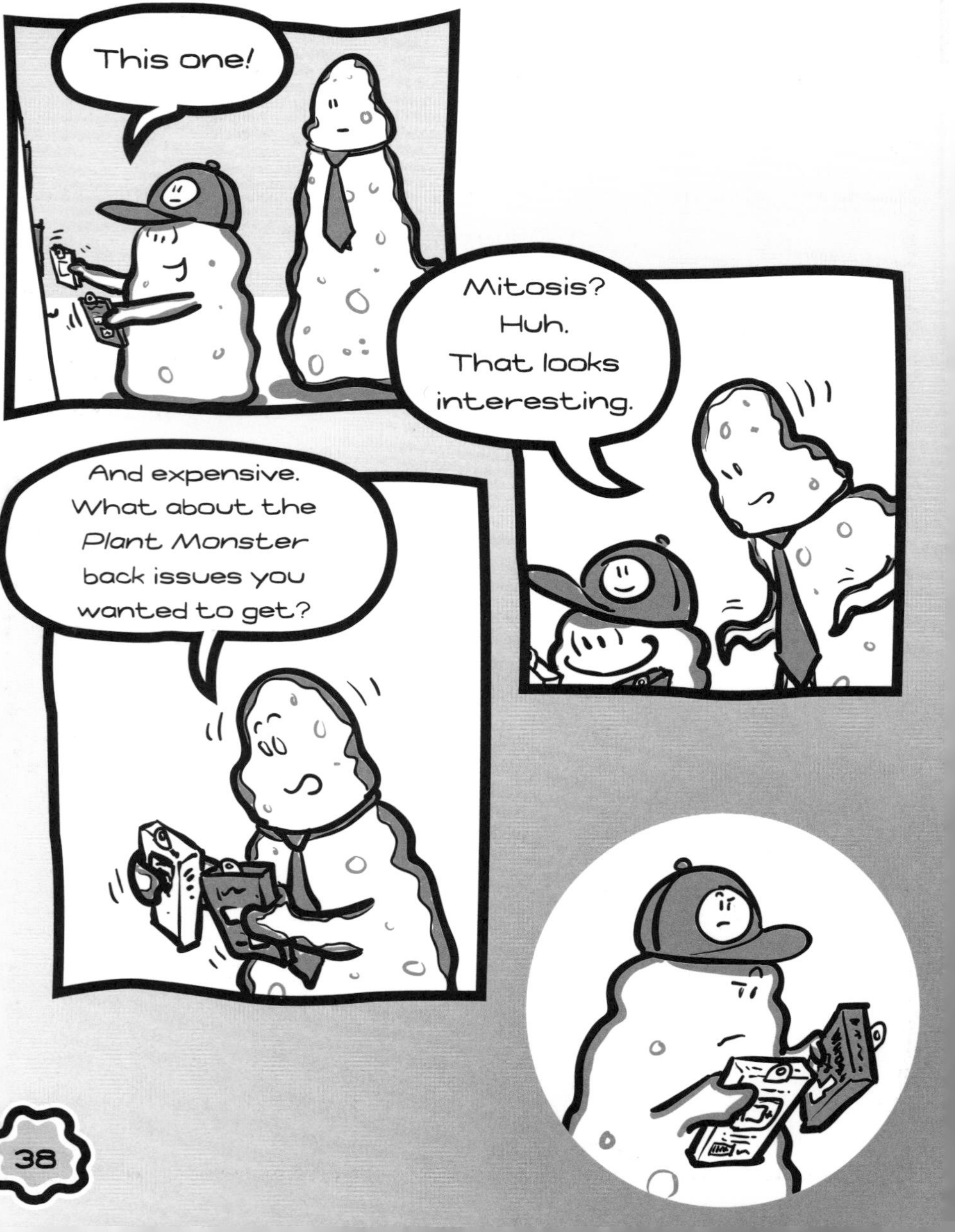
This one!
Mitosis? Huh. That looks interesting.
And expensive. What about the *Plant Monster* back issues you wanted to get?

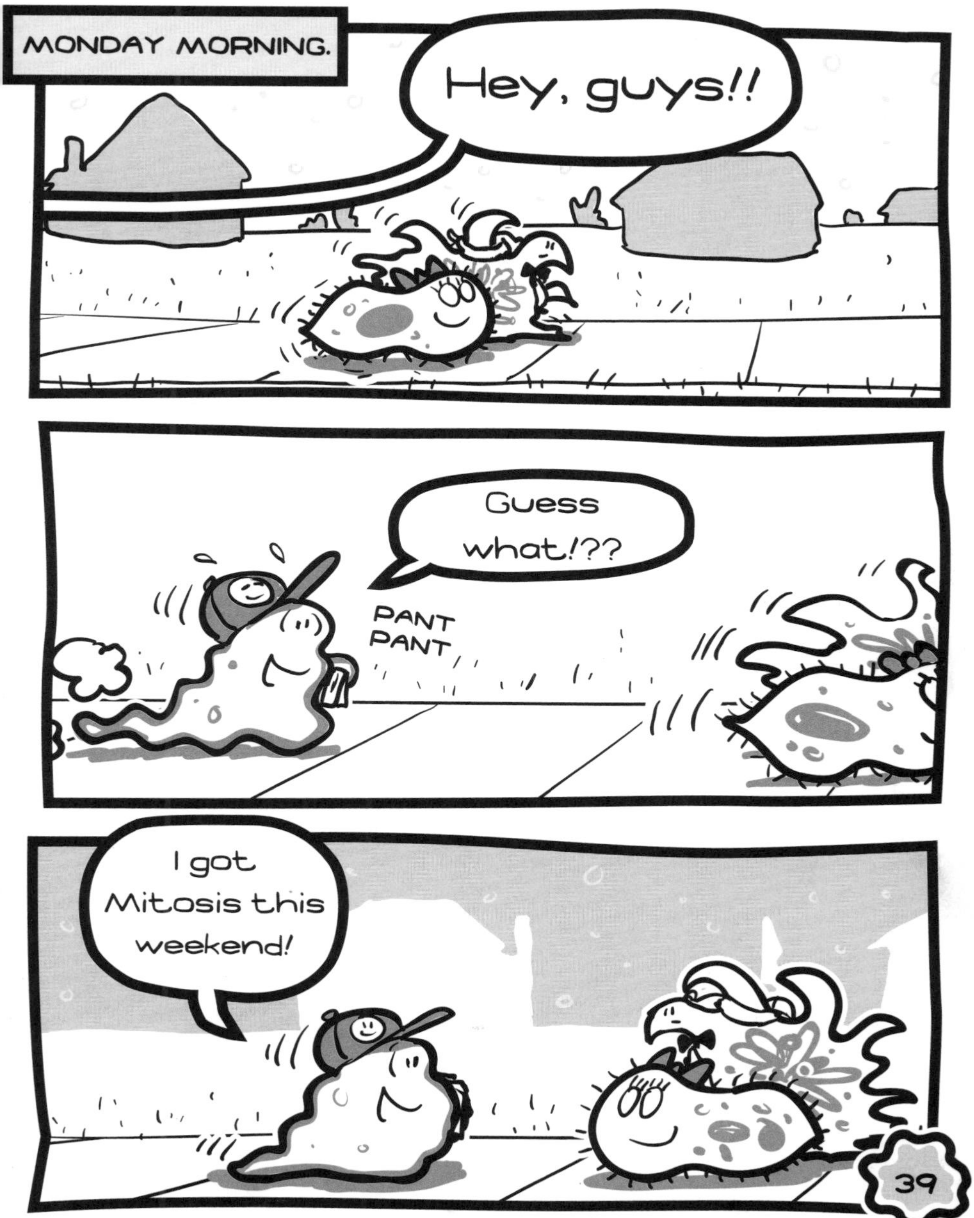
MONDAY MORNING.
Hey, guys!!
Guess what!??
PANT PANT
I got Mitosis this weekend!
39

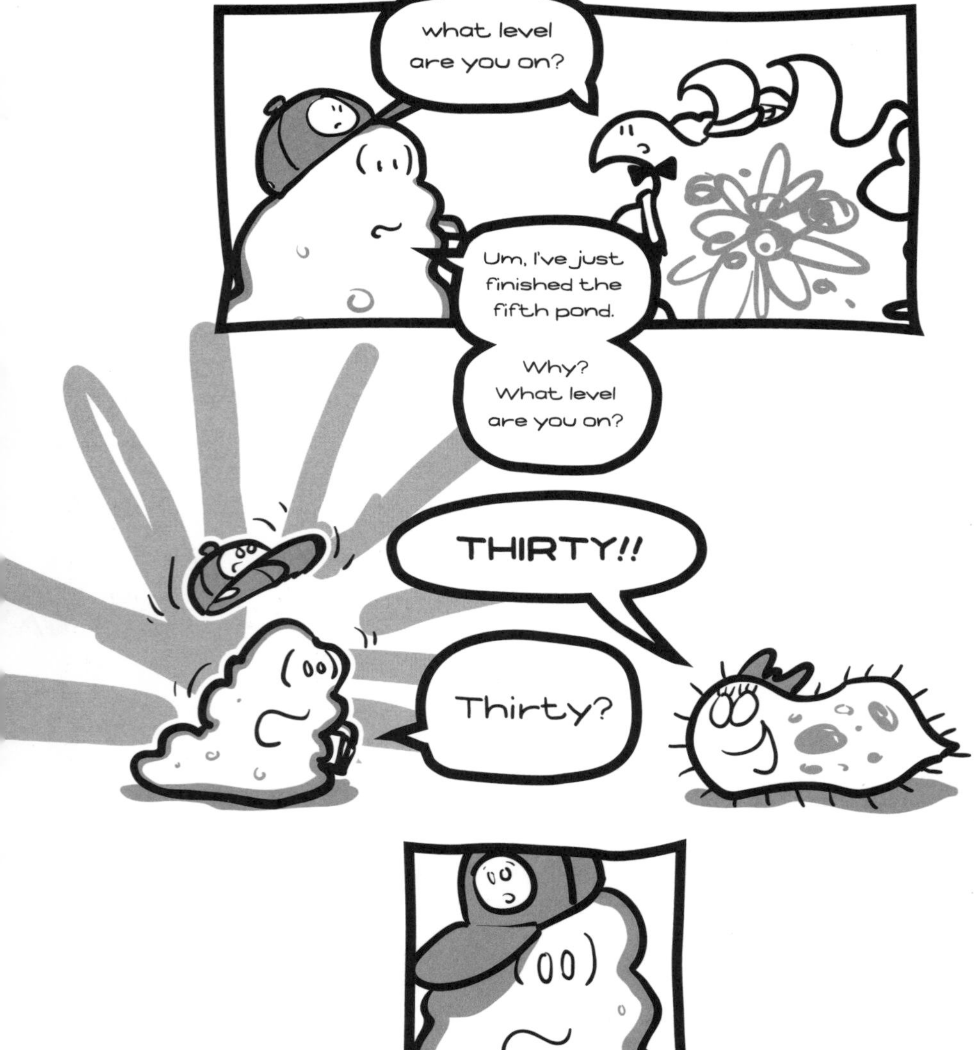
what level are you on?
Um, I've just finished the fifth pond.
Why? What level are you on?
THIRTY!!
Thirty?

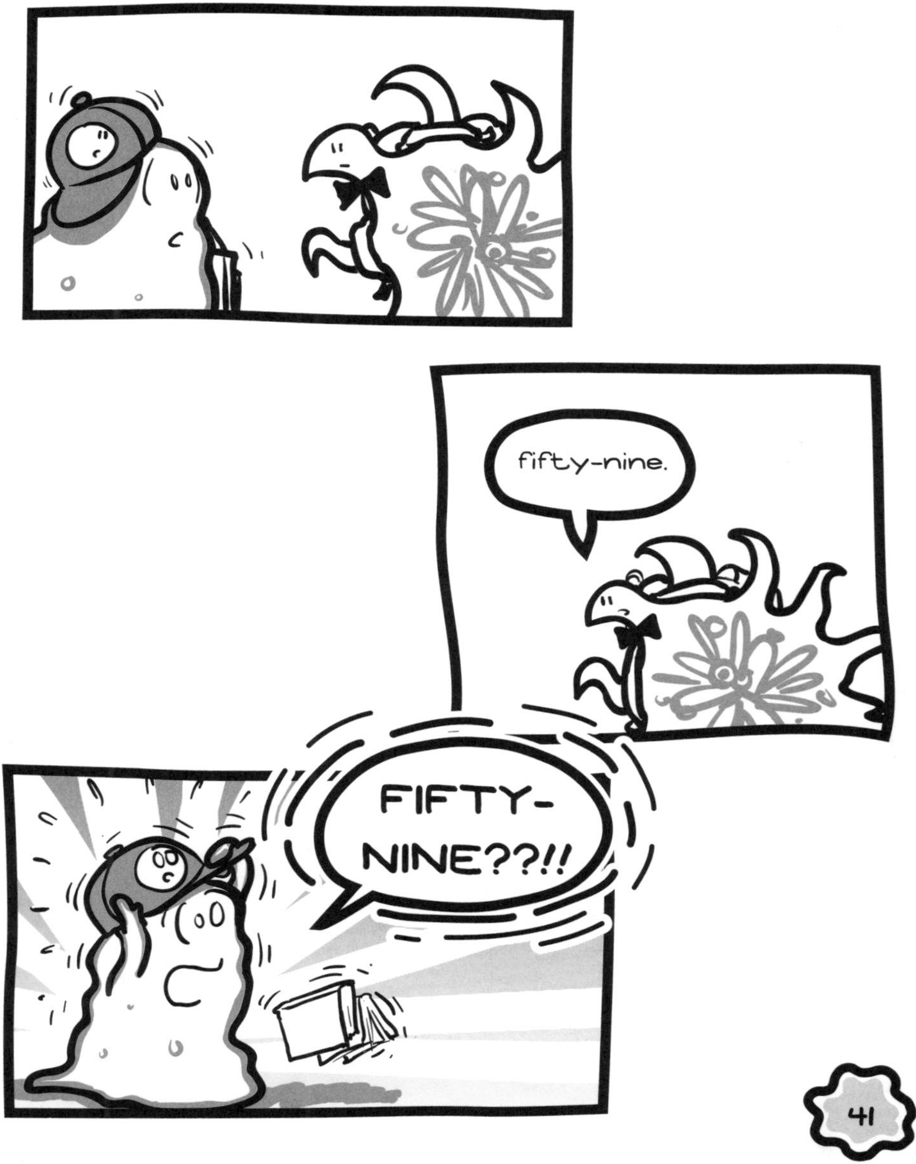
fifty-nine.
FIFTY-NINE??!!

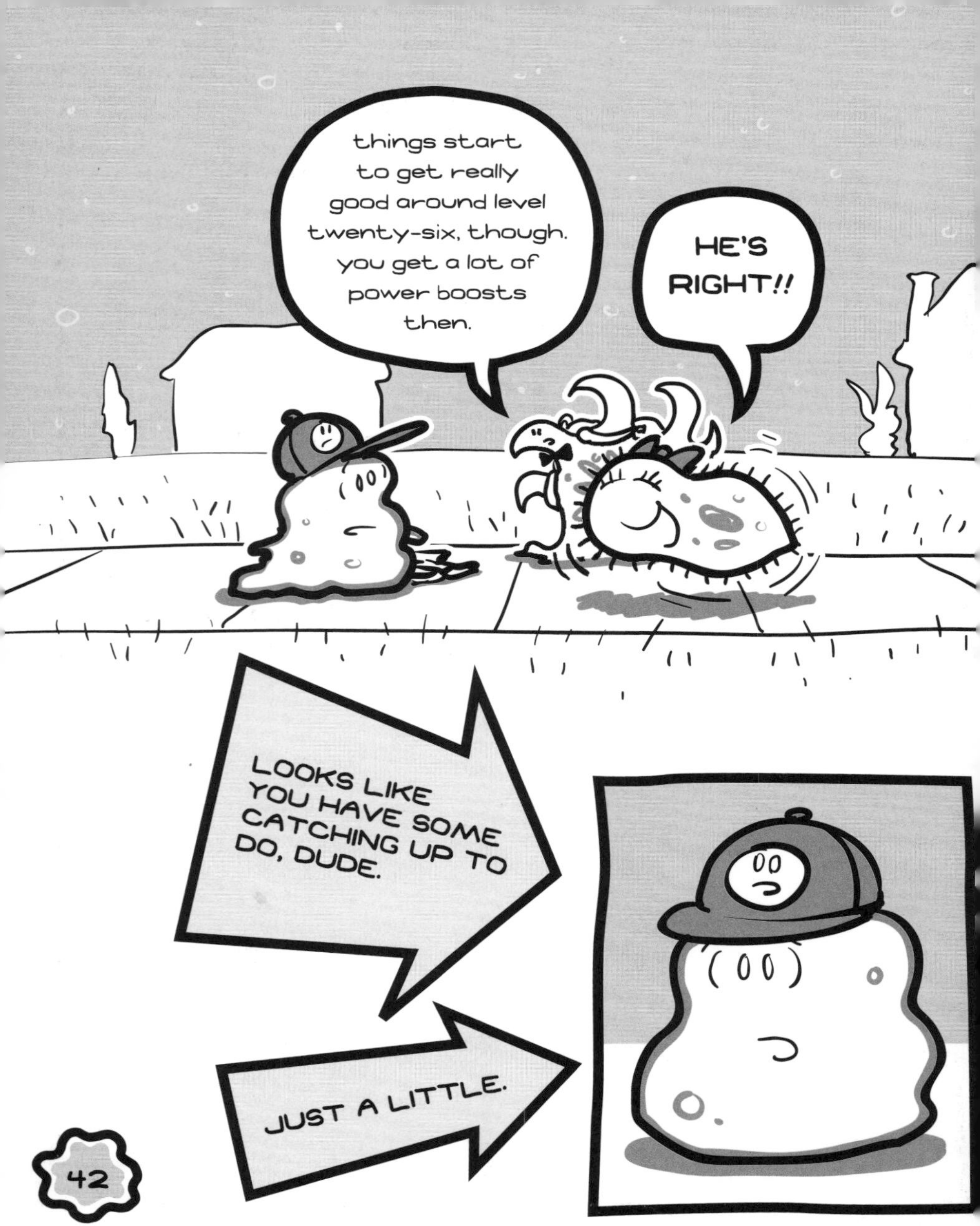
things start to get really good around level twenty-six, though. you get a lot of power boosts then.
HE'S RIGHT!!
LOOKS LIKE YOU HAVE SOME CATCHING UP TO DO, DUDE.
JUST A LITTLE.

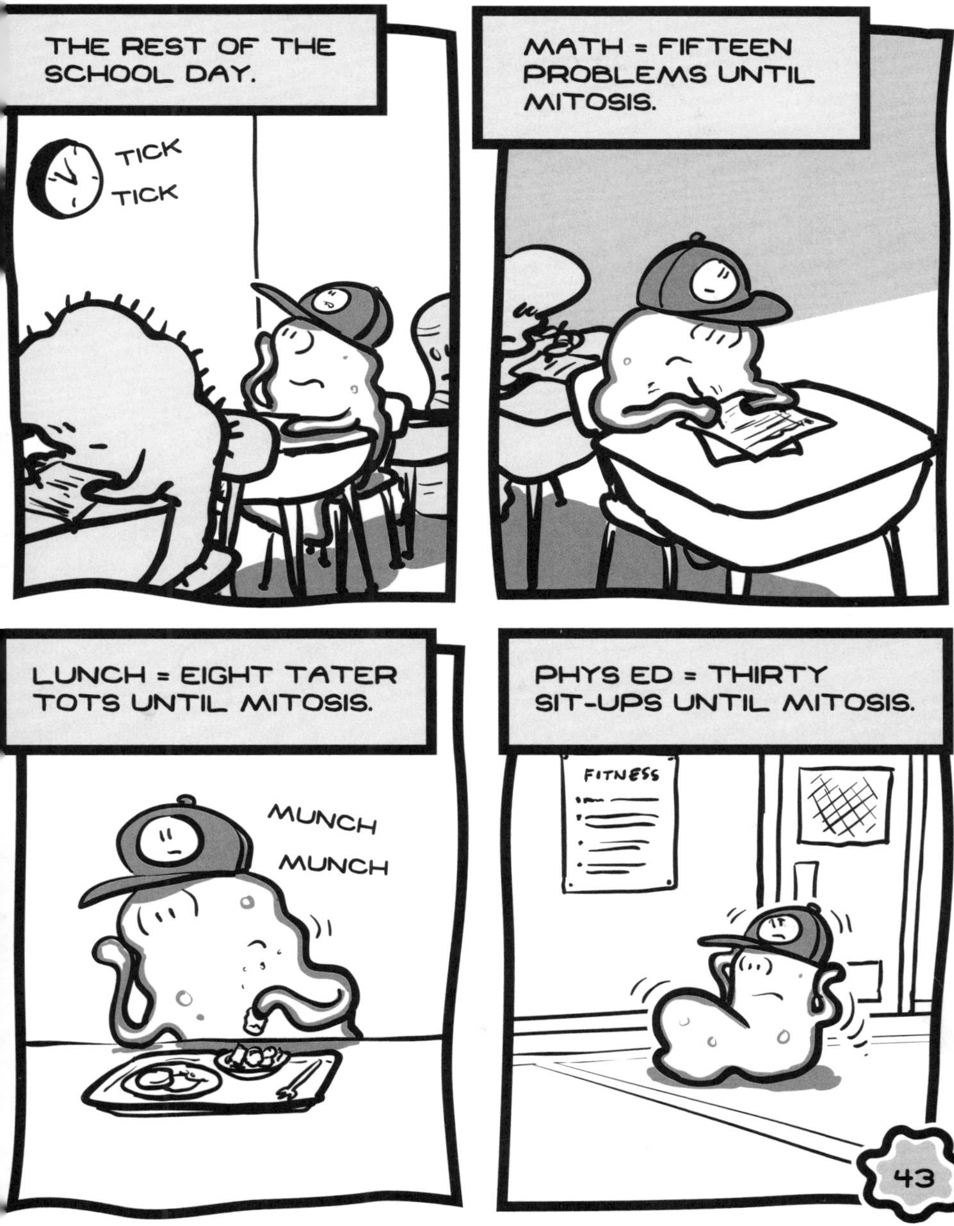
THE REST OF THE SCHOOL DAY.
TICK
TICK
MATH = FIFTEEN PROBLEMS UNTIL MITOSIS.
LUNCH = EIGHT TATER TOTS UNTIL MITOSIS.
MUNCH
MUNCH
PHYS ED = THIRTY SIT-UPS UNTIL MITOSIS.
FITNESS

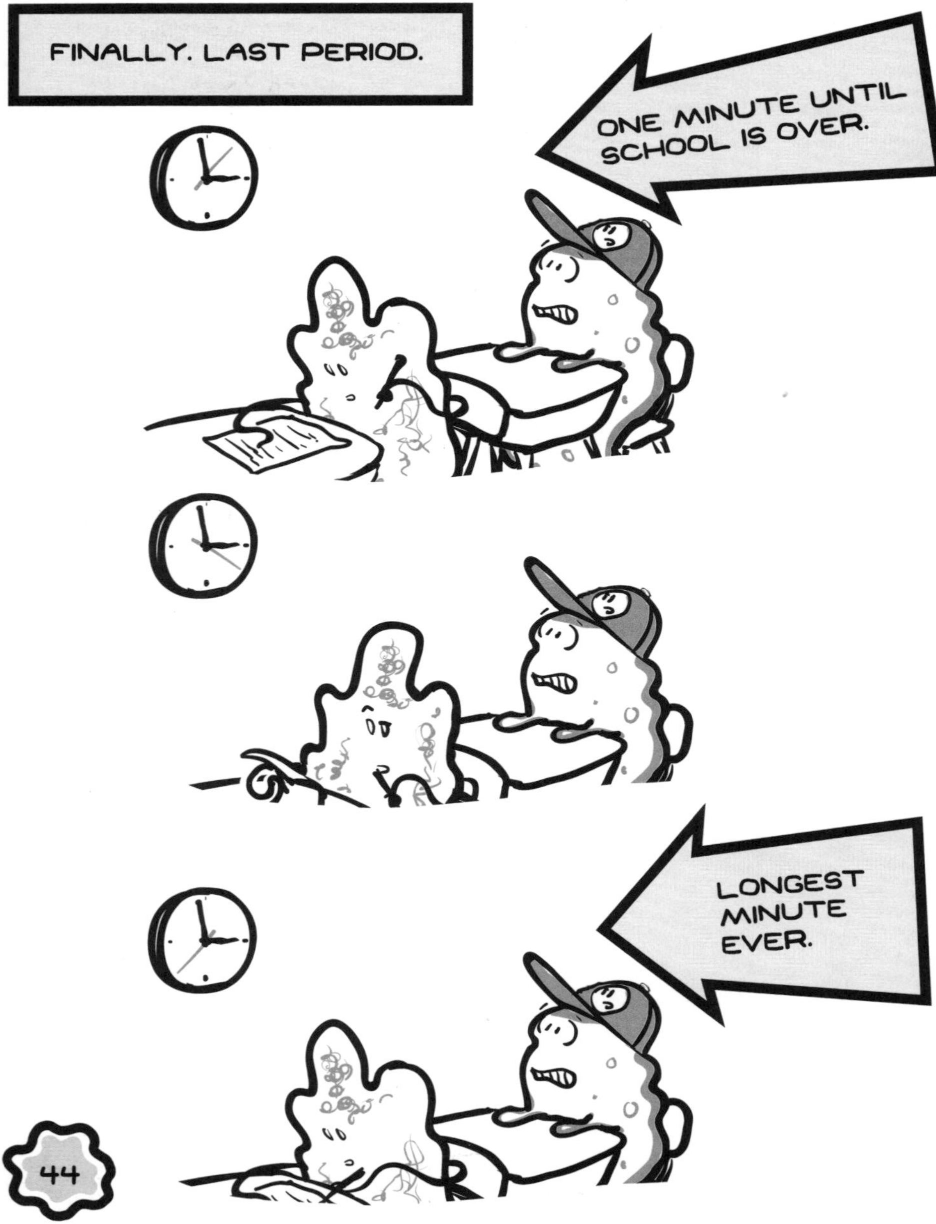
FINALLY. LAST PERIOD.
ONE MINUTE UNTIL SCHOOL IS OVER.
LONGEST MINUTE EVER.

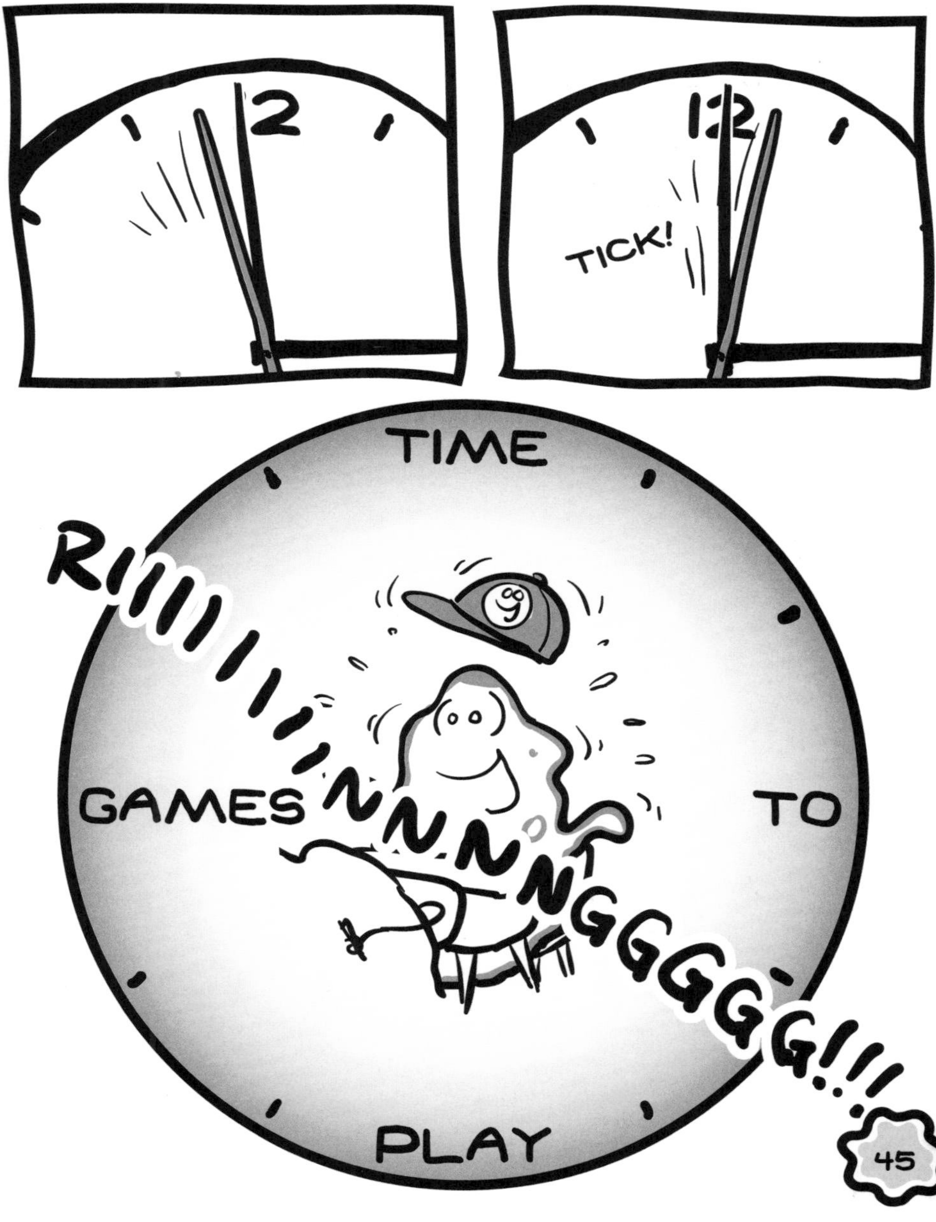
TICK!
TIME
GAMES
TO
PLAY
RIIIIIIIINNNNGGGGGG!!!!

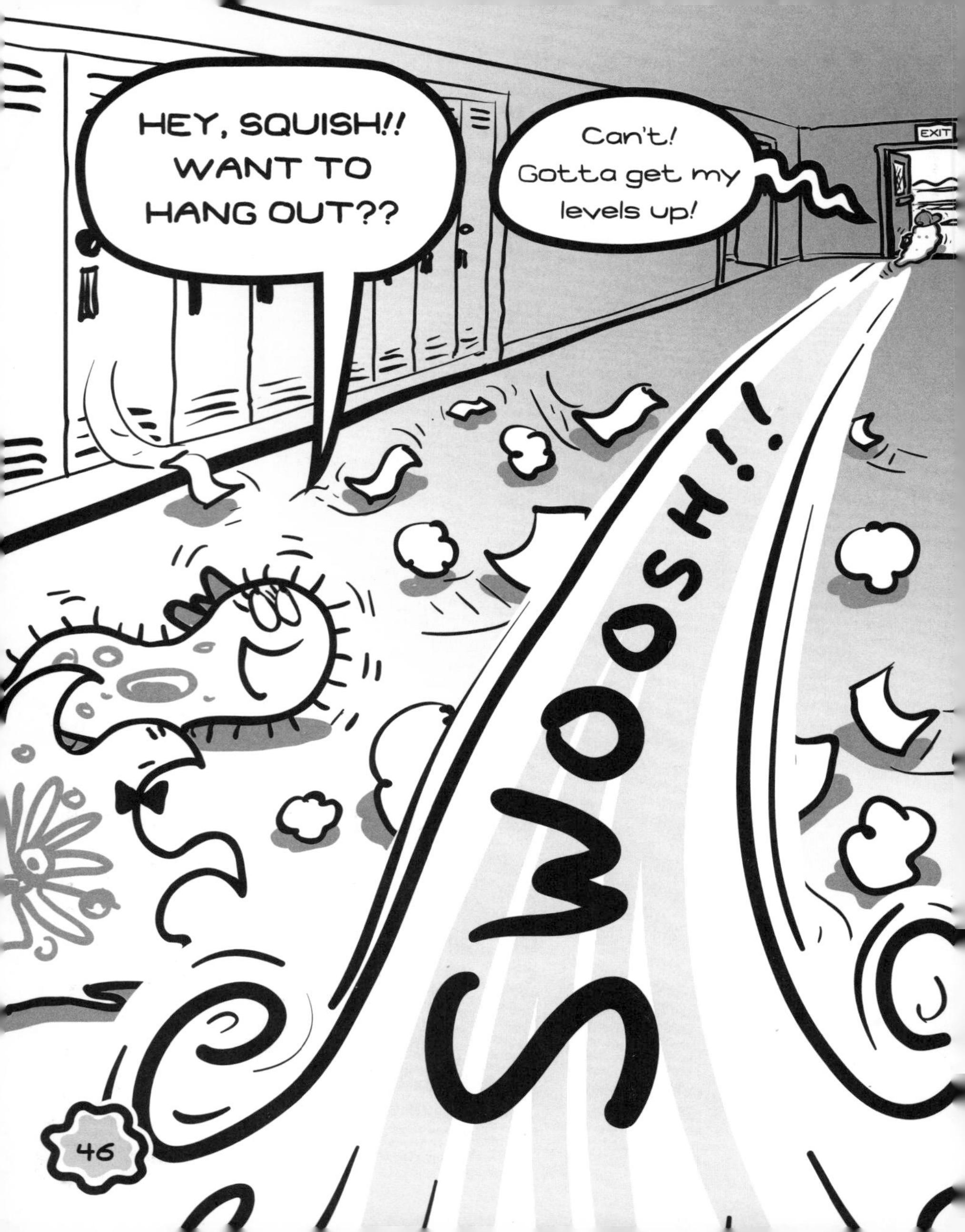
HEY, SQUISH!! WANT TO HANG OUT??
Can't! Gotta get my levels up!
EXIT
SWOOSH!!

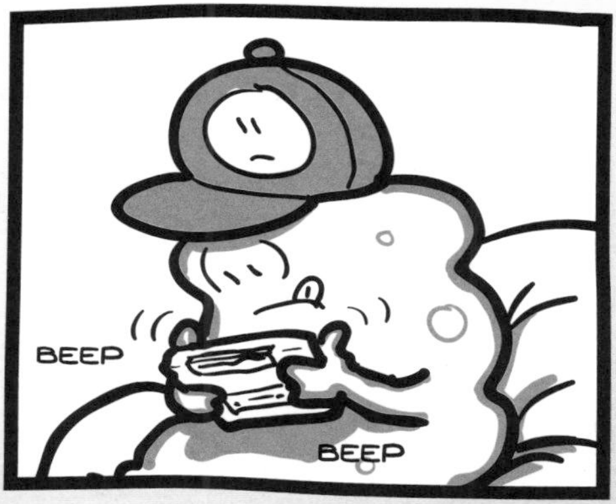
BEEP
BEEP

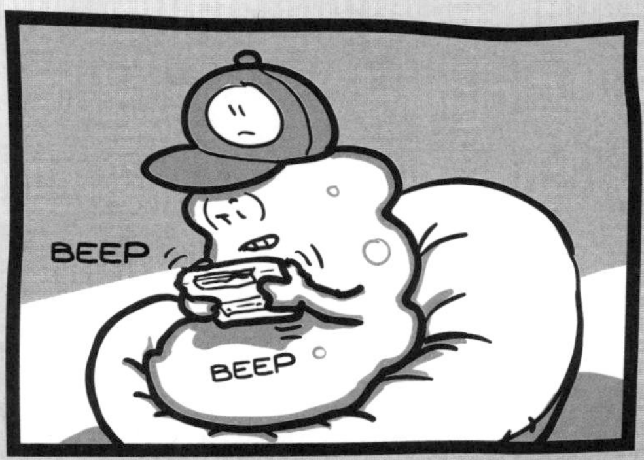
BEEP
BEEP

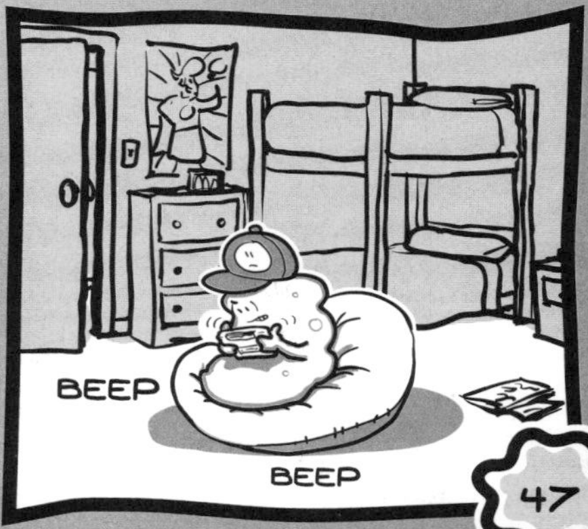
BEEP
BEEP

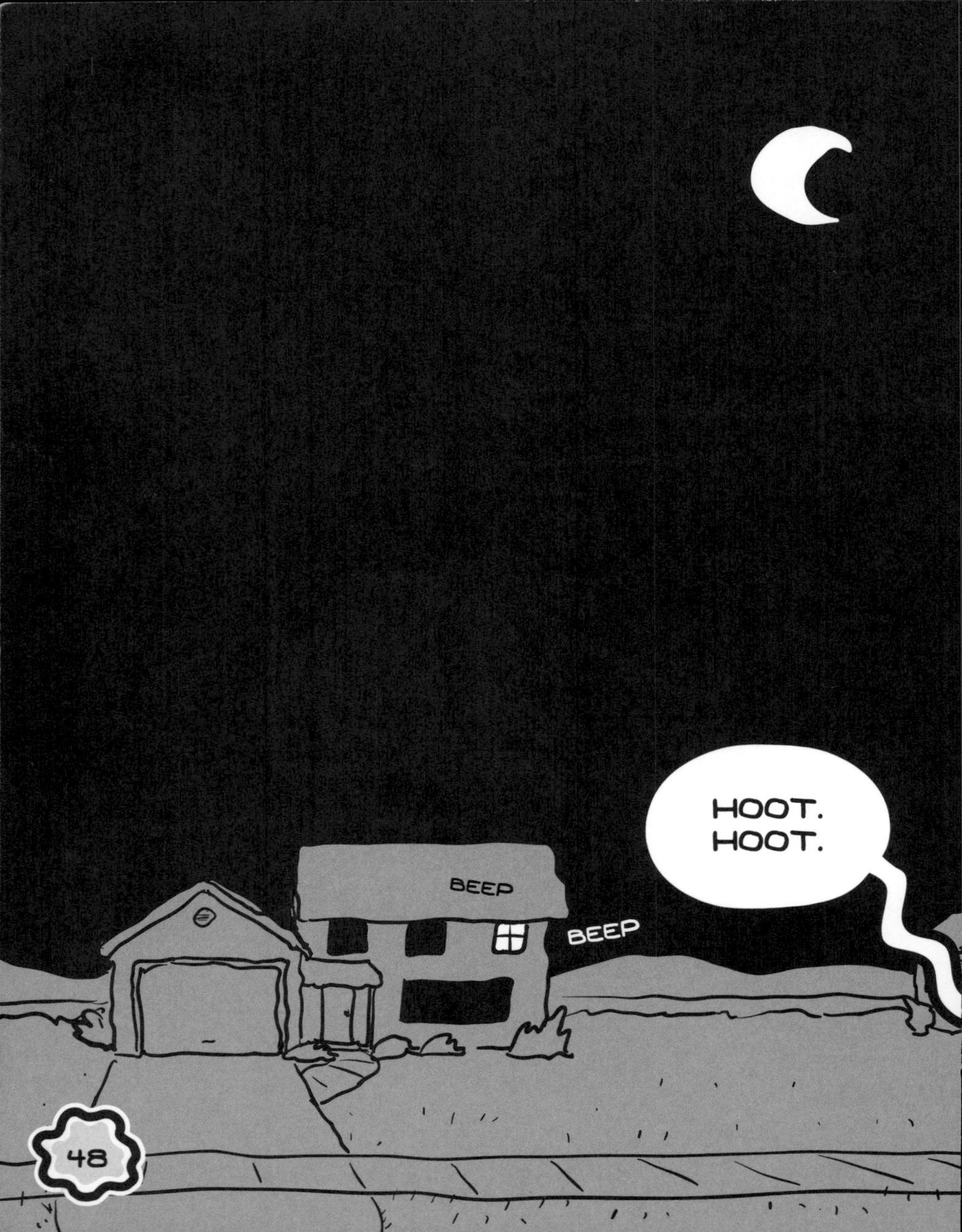
BEEP
BEEP
HOOT. HOOT.

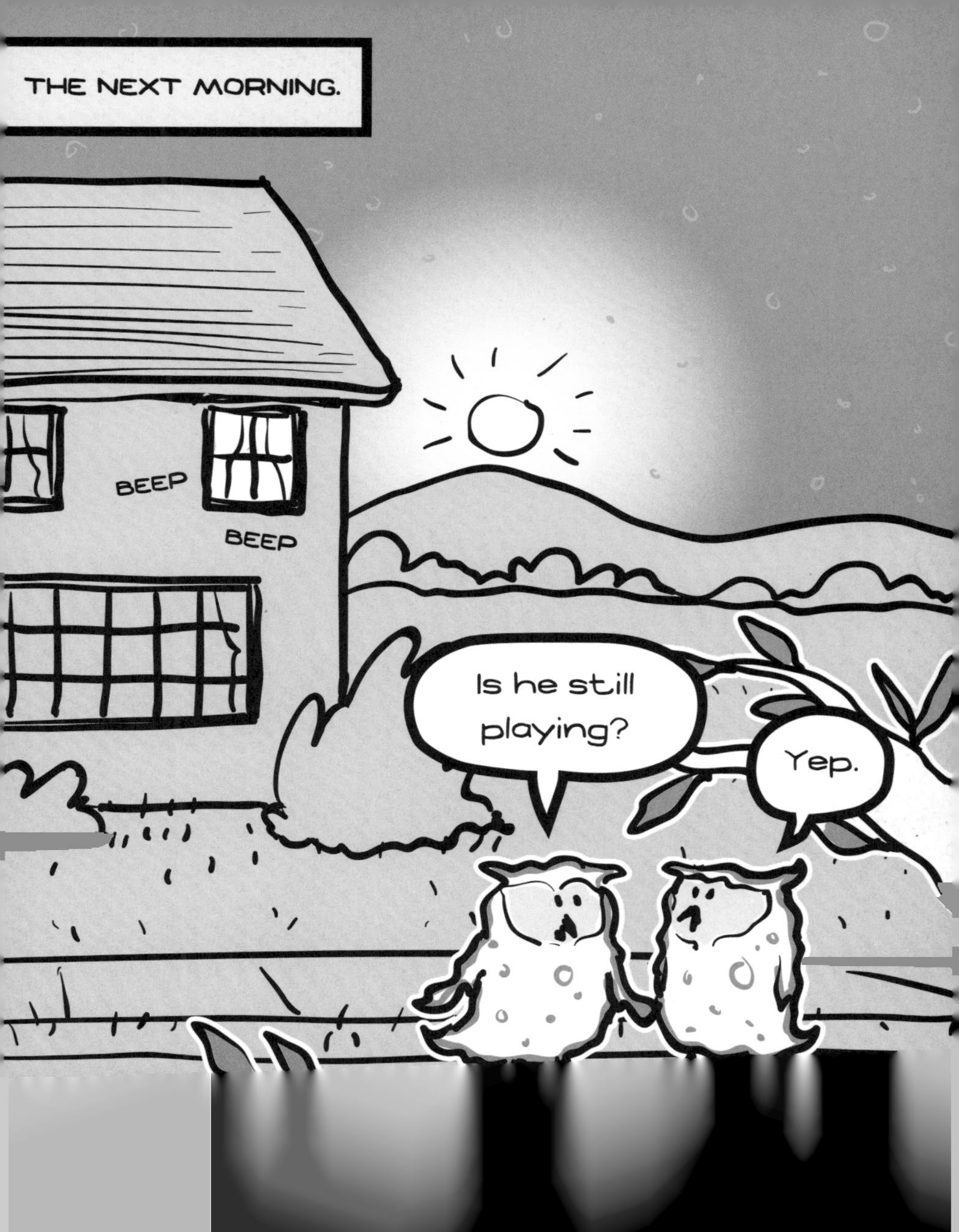
THE NEXT MORNING.
BEEP
BEEP
Is he still playing?
Yep.

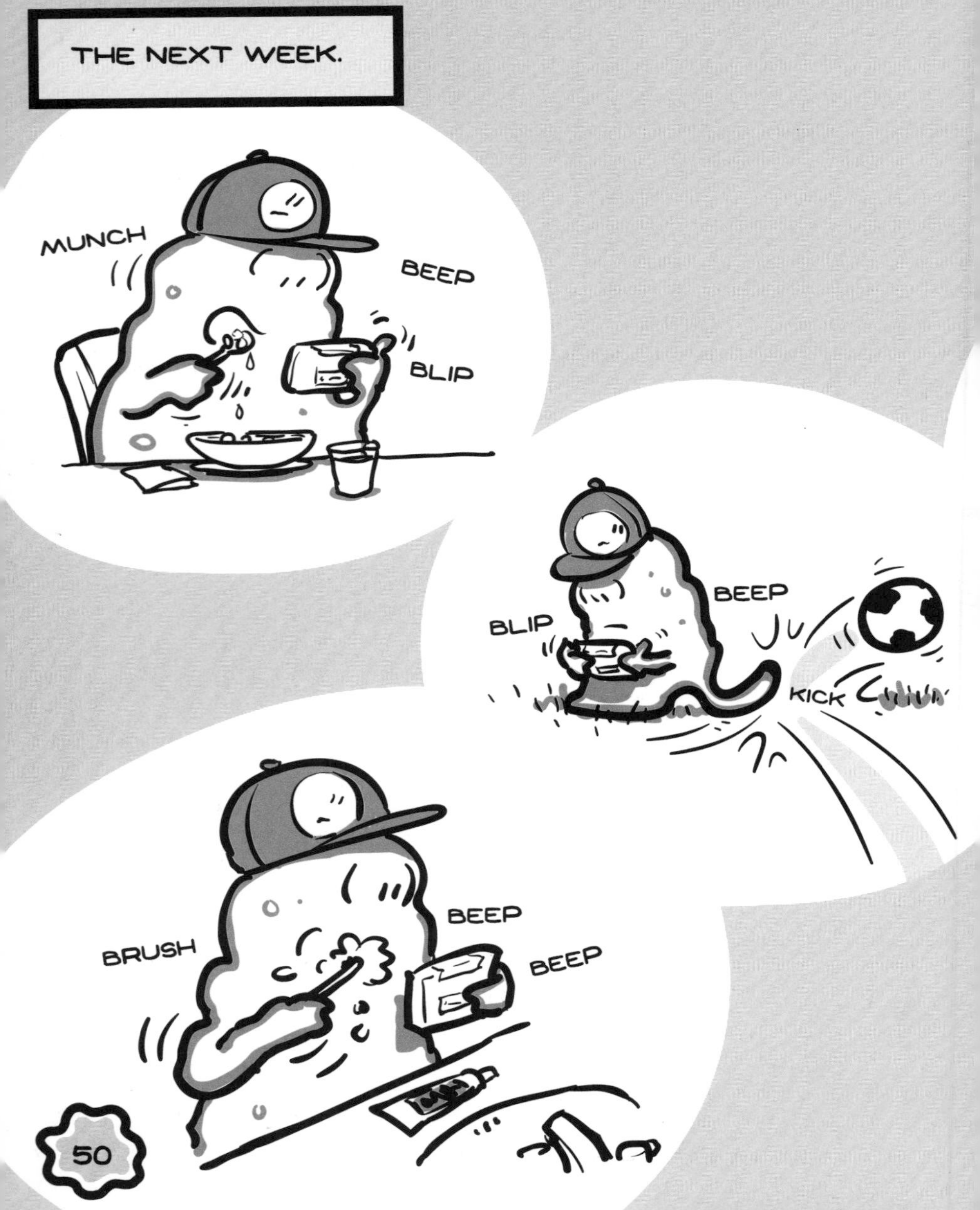
THE NEXT WEEK.
MUNCH
BEEP
BLIP
BLIP
BEEP
KICK
BRUSH
BEEP
BEEP

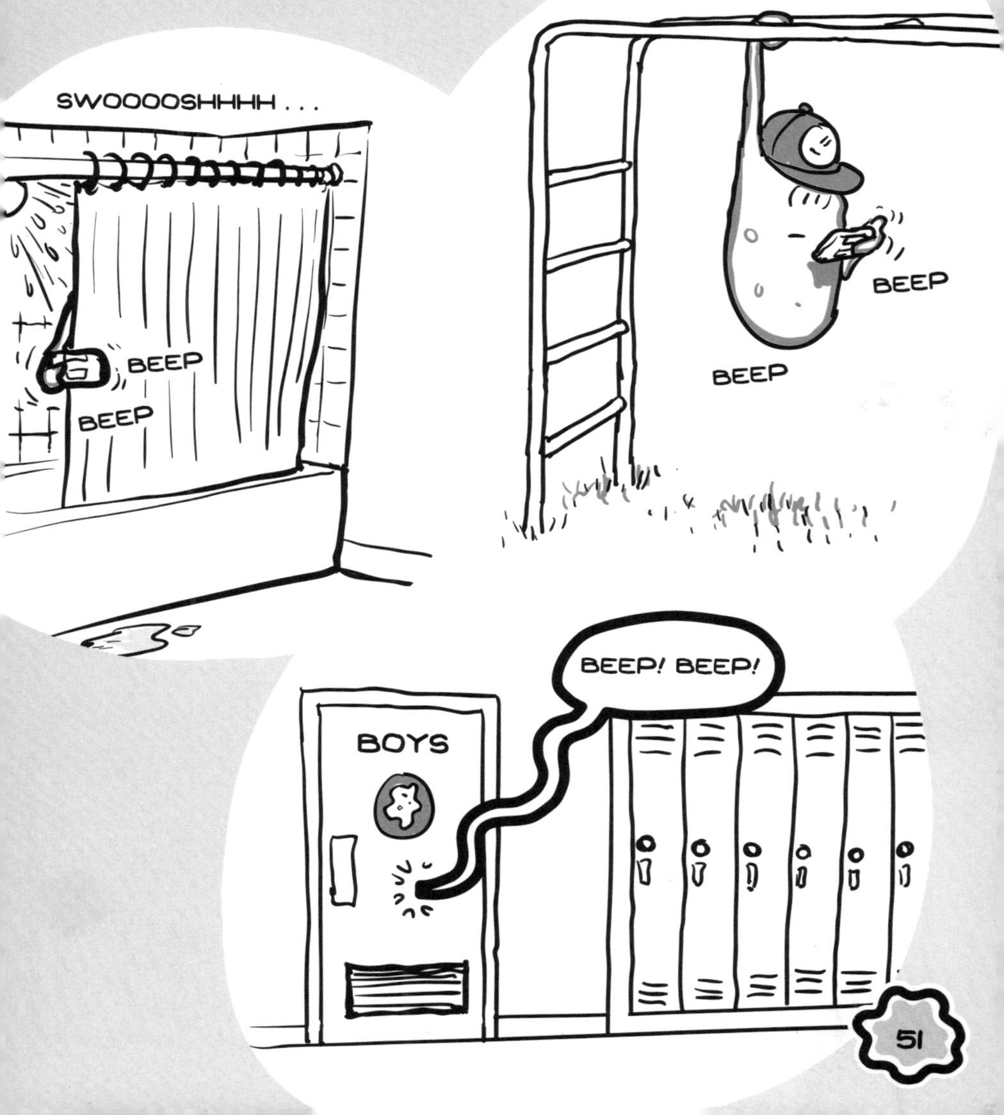

SWOOOOSHHHH . . .
BEEP
BEEP
BEEP
BEEP
BEEP! BEEP!
BOYS

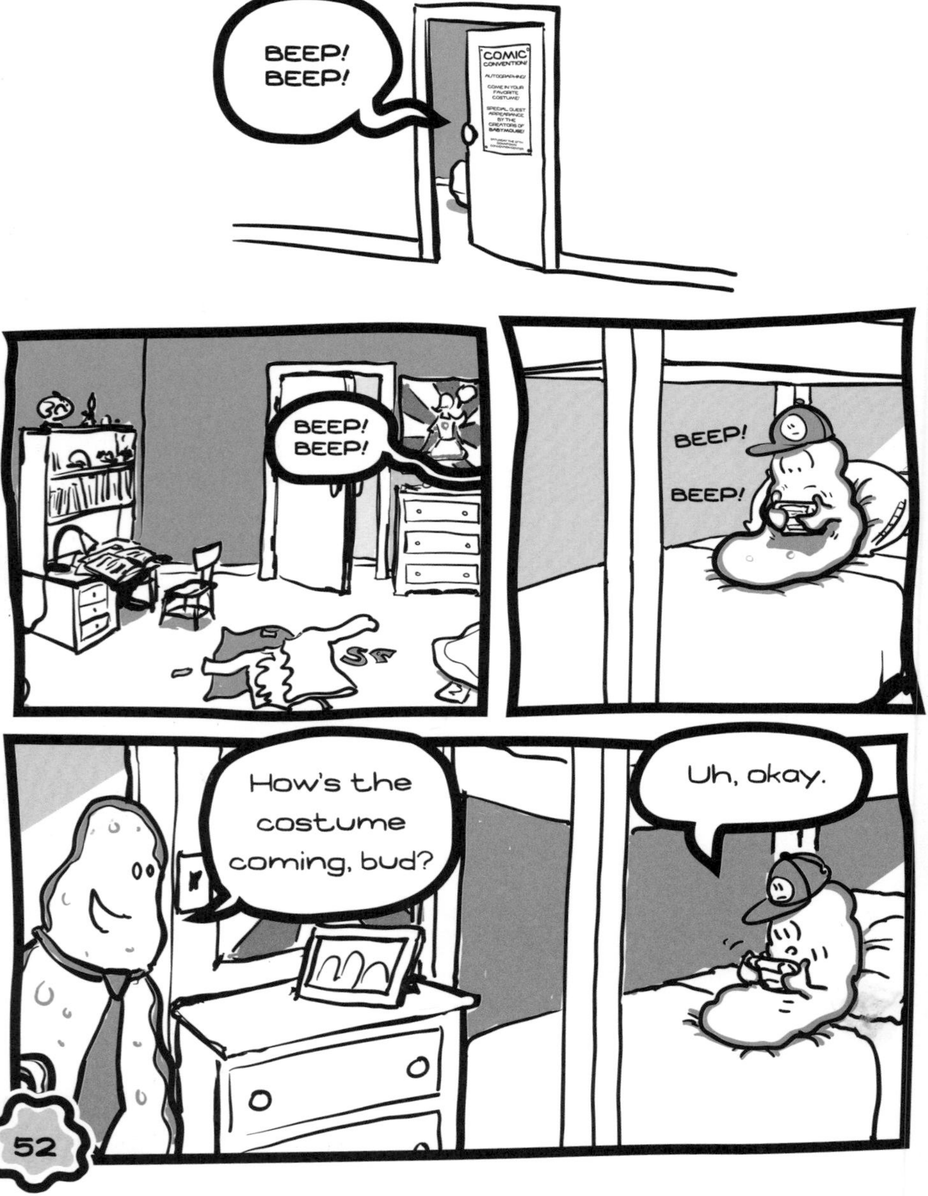
BEEP! BEEP!
COMIC CONVENTION!
AUTOGRAPHING!
COME IN YOUR FAVORITE COSTUME!
SPECIAL GUEST APPEARANCE BY THE CREATORS OF BABYMOUSE!
BEEP! BEEP!
BEEP!
BEEP!
How's the costume coming, bud?
Uh, okay.

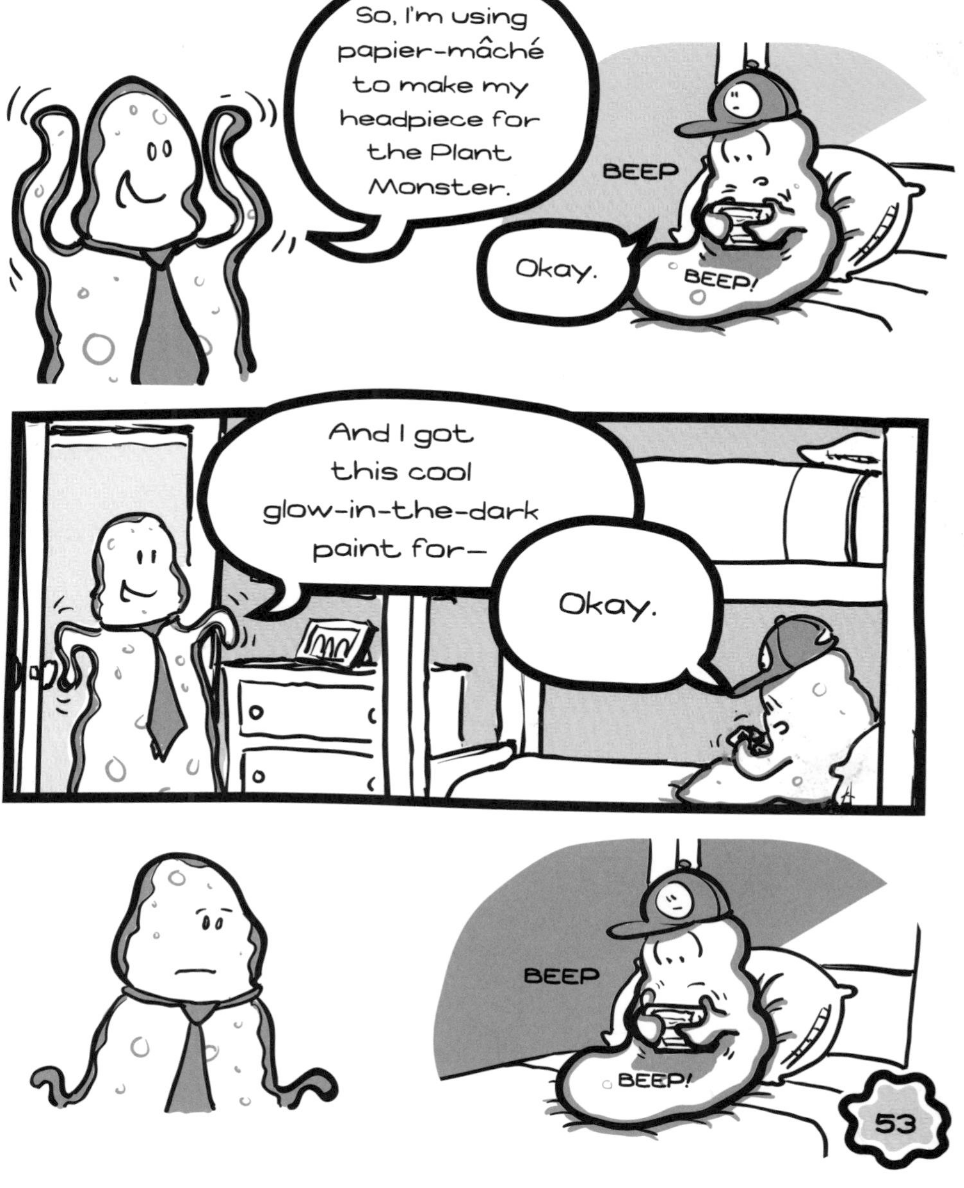
So, I'm using papier-mâché to make my headpiece for the Plant Monster.
BEEP
Okay.
BEEP!
And I got this cool glow-in-the-dark paint for—
Okay.
BEEP
BEEP!

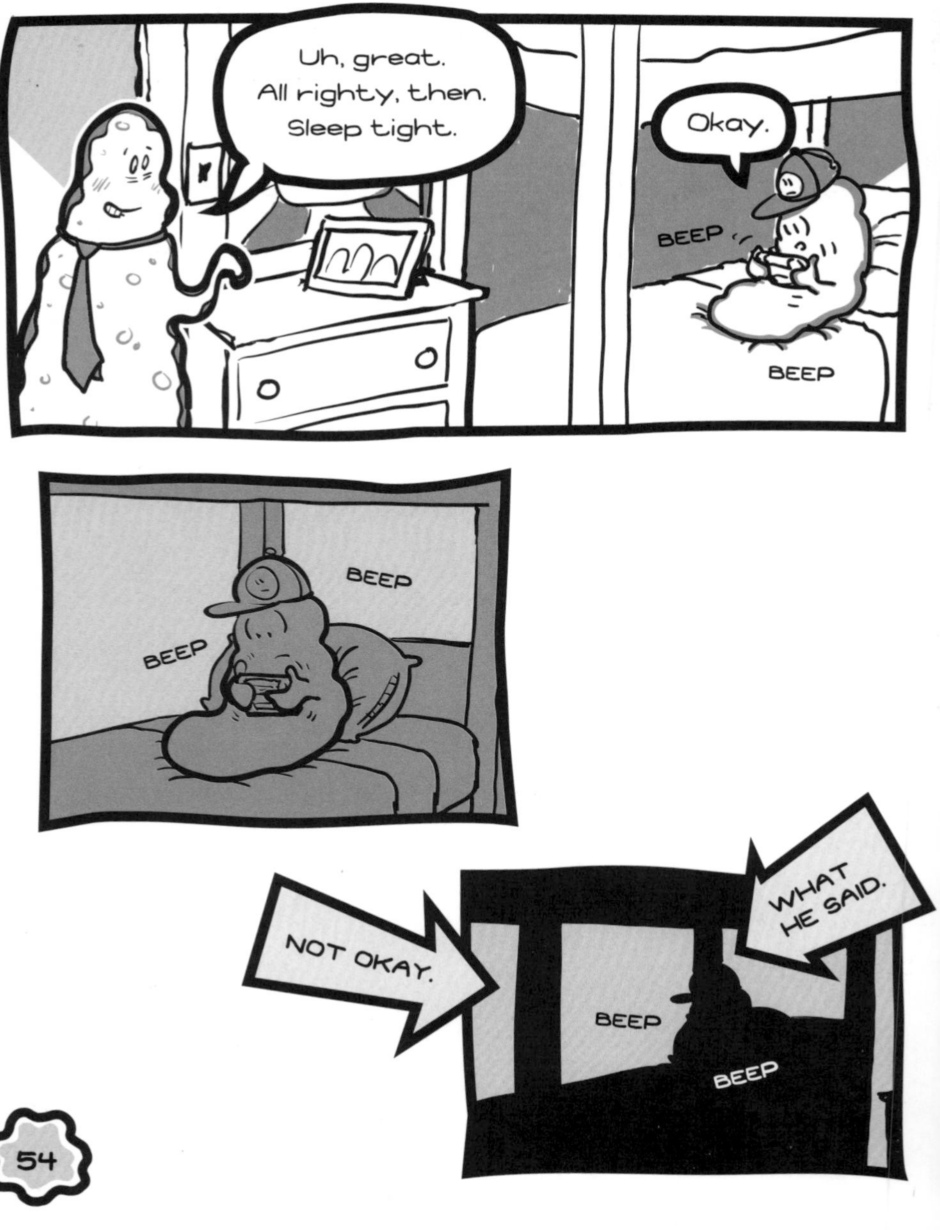
Uh, great.
All righty, then.
Sleep tight.
Okay.
BEEP
BEEP
BEEP
BEEP
NOT OKAY.
WHAT HE SAID.
BEEP
BEEP

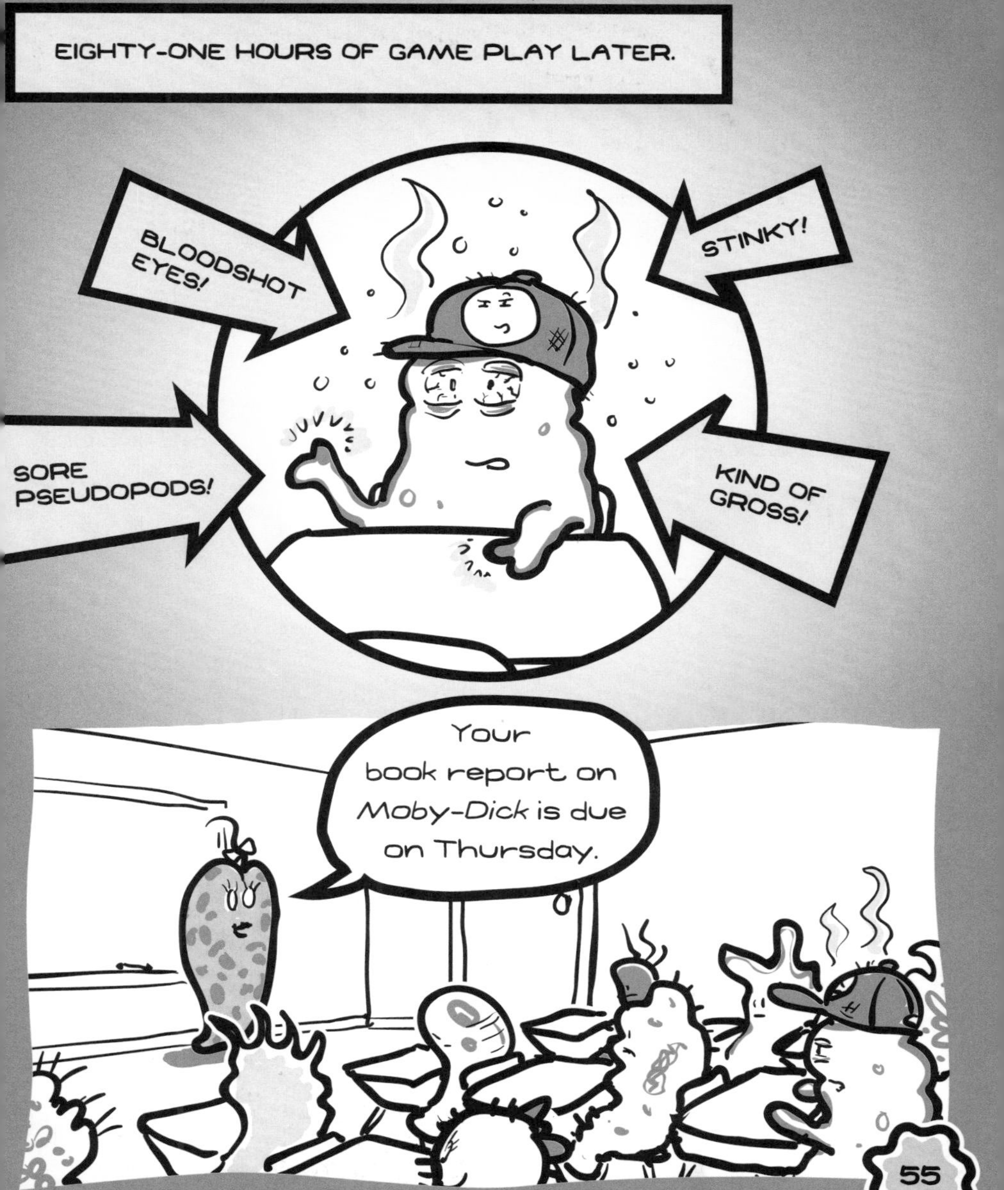
EIGHTY-ONE HOURS OF GAME PLAY LATER.
BLOODSHOT EYES!
STINKY!
SORE PSEUDOPODS!
KIND OF GROSS!
Your book report on *Moby-Dick* is due on Thursday.

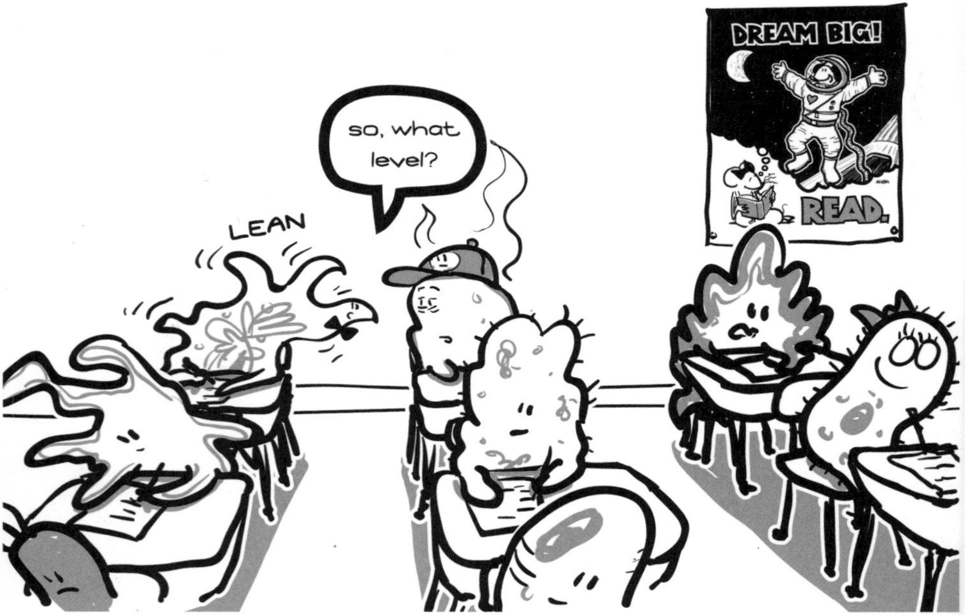
DREAM BIG!
READ.
LEAN
so, what level?

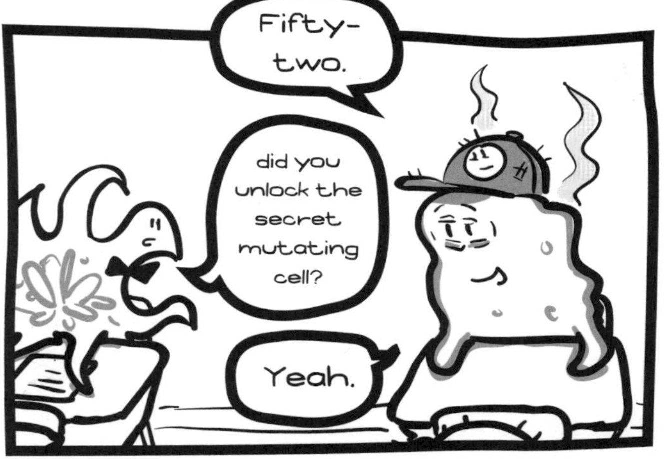
Fifty-two.
did you unlock the secret mutating cell?
Yeah.

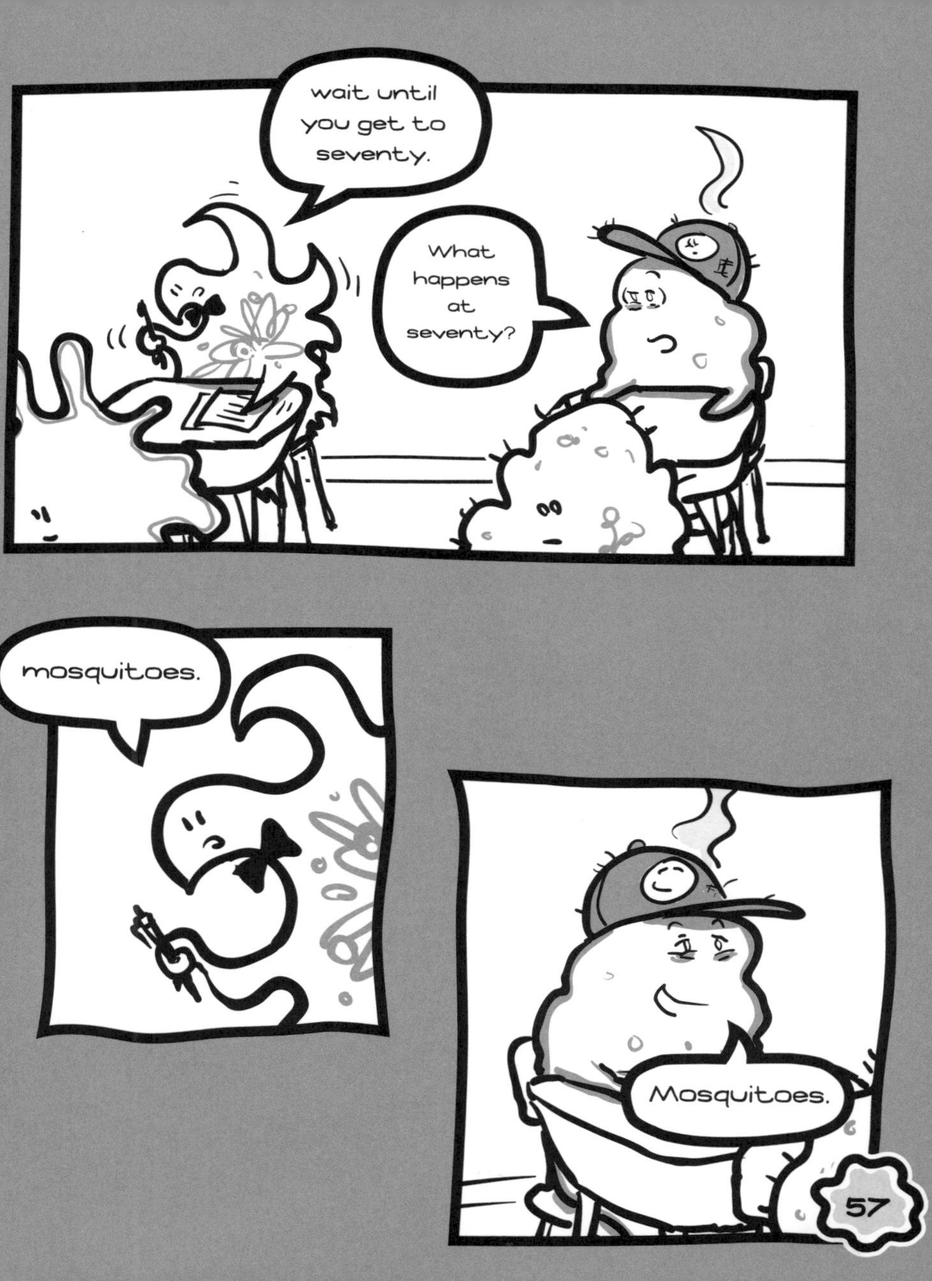
wait until you get to seventy.
What happens at seventy?
mosquitoes.
Mosquitoes.

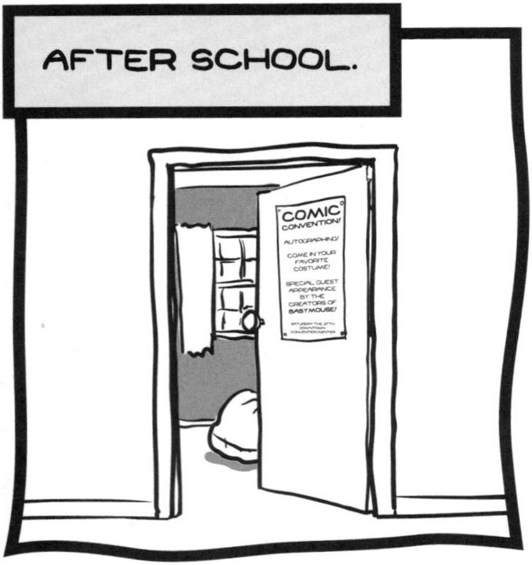
AFTER SCHOOL.
COMIC CONVENTION!
AUTOGRAPHING!
COME IN YOUR FAVORITE COSTUME!
SPECIAL GUEST APPEARANCE BY THE CREATORS OF BABYMOUSE!
SATURDAY THE 27TH
DOWNTOWN
CONVENTION CENTER

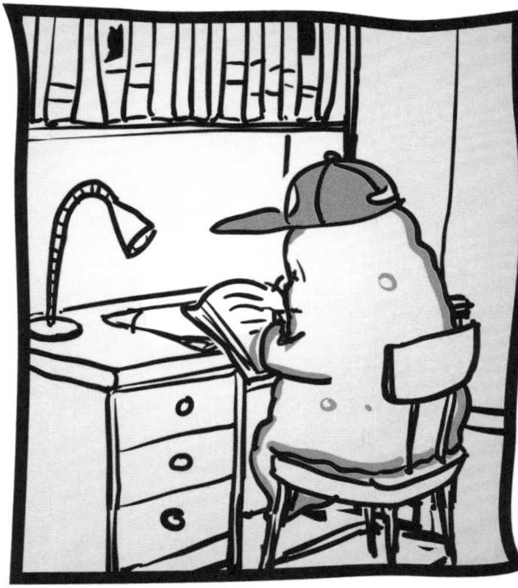

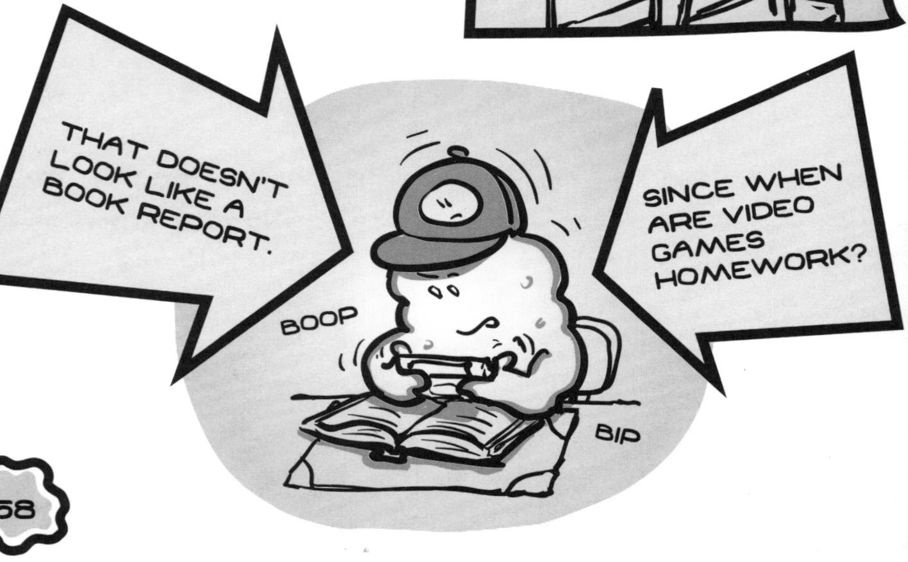
THAT DOESN'T LOOK LIKE A BOOK REPORT.
SINCE WHEN ARE VIDEO GAMES HOMEWORK?
BOOP
BIP

CLOSE-UP OF GAME PLAY.
589450
BLOOP!
LEVEL 66
590150
BIP!
591000
BEEP!
SWOOSH!
GALAXY EFFECT!
596500
BIP!
LEVEL 67
597200
BEEP!

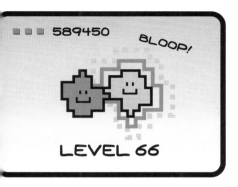

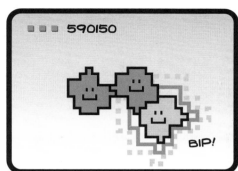

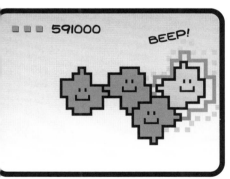

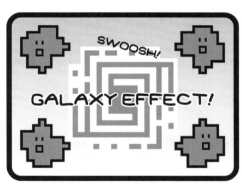

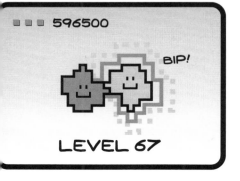

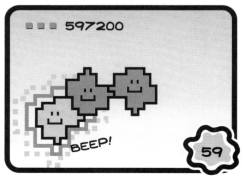

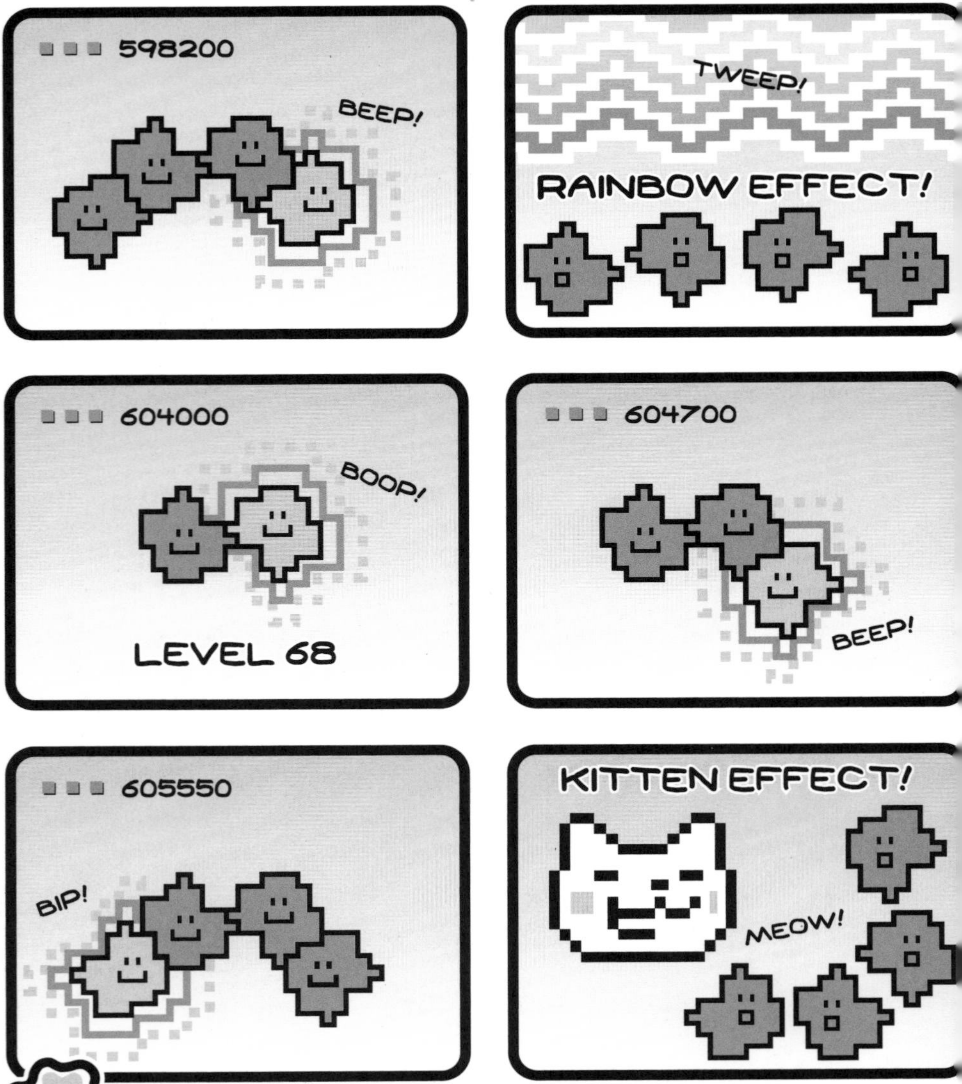
598200
BEEP!
TWEEP!
RAINBOW EFFECT!
604000
BOOP!
LEVEL 68
604700
BEEP!
605550
BIP!
KITTEN EFFECT!
MEOW!

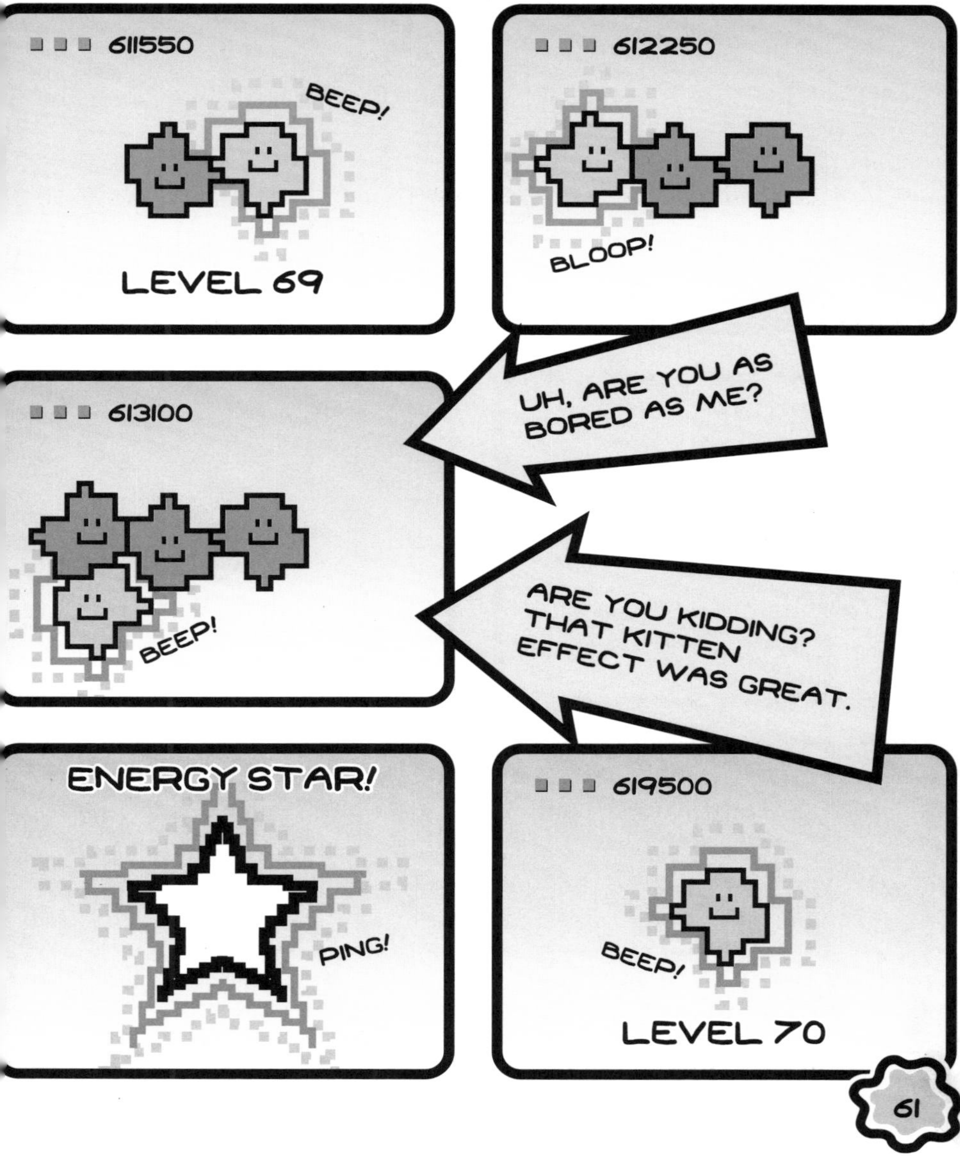
611550
BEEP!
LEVEL 69
612250
BLOOP!
UH, ARE YOU AS BORED AS ME?
613100
BEEP!
ARE YOU KIDDING? THAT KITTEN EFFECT WAS GREAT.
ENERGY STAR!
PING!
619500
BEEP!
LEVEL 70

Finally.

Okay. Let's see how bad those mosquitoes are.

619500

BZZZZ . . .

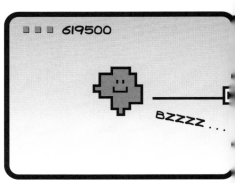

619500

BZZZZ . . .

BZZZZ . . .

CLICK

TAP

BOUNCE

BZZZ

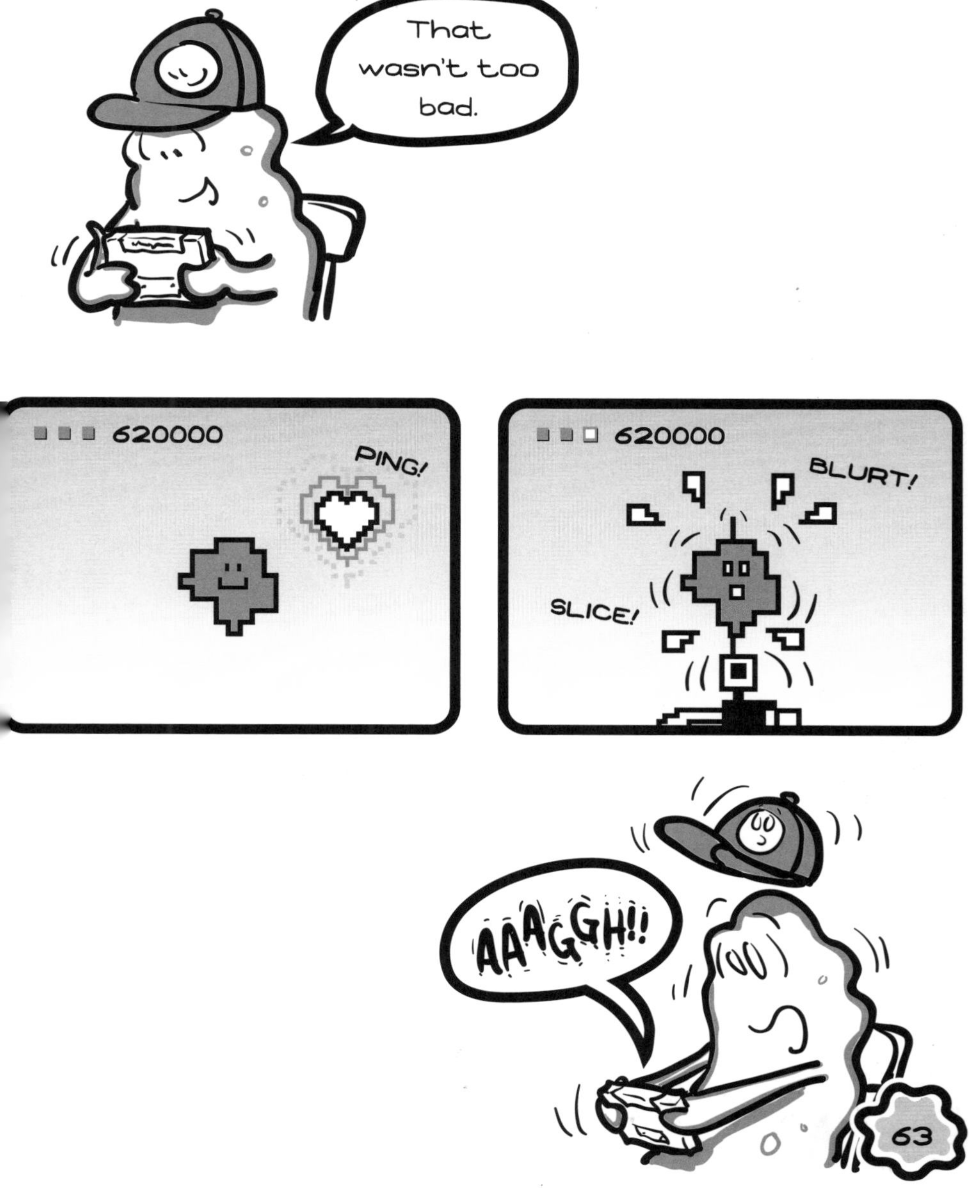

That wasn't too bad.
620000
PING!
620000
BLURT!
SLICE!
AAAGGH!!

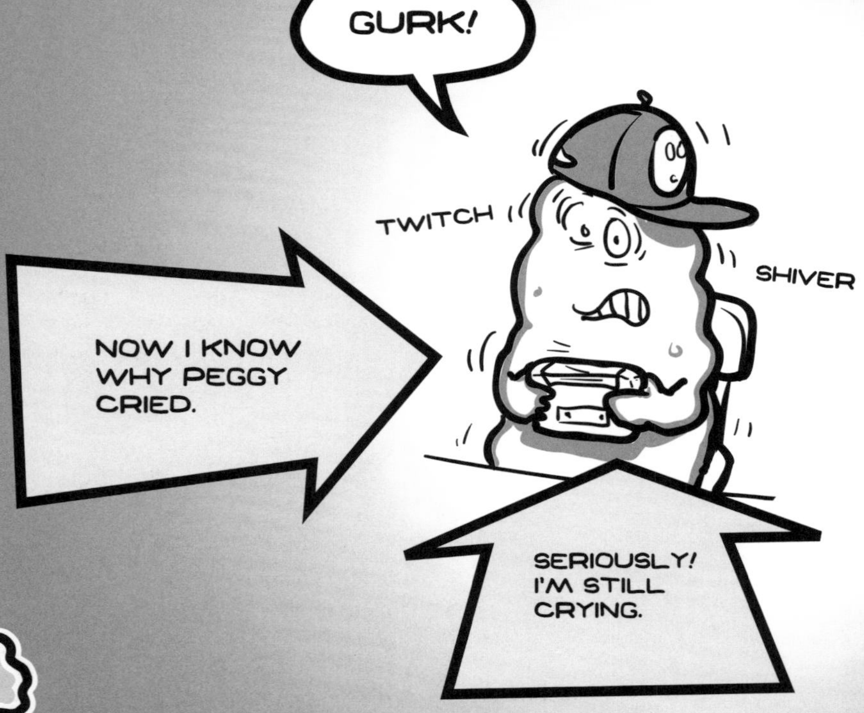
GURK!
TWITCH
SHIVER
NOW I KNOW WHY PEGGY CRIED.
SERIOUSLY! I'M STILL CRYING.

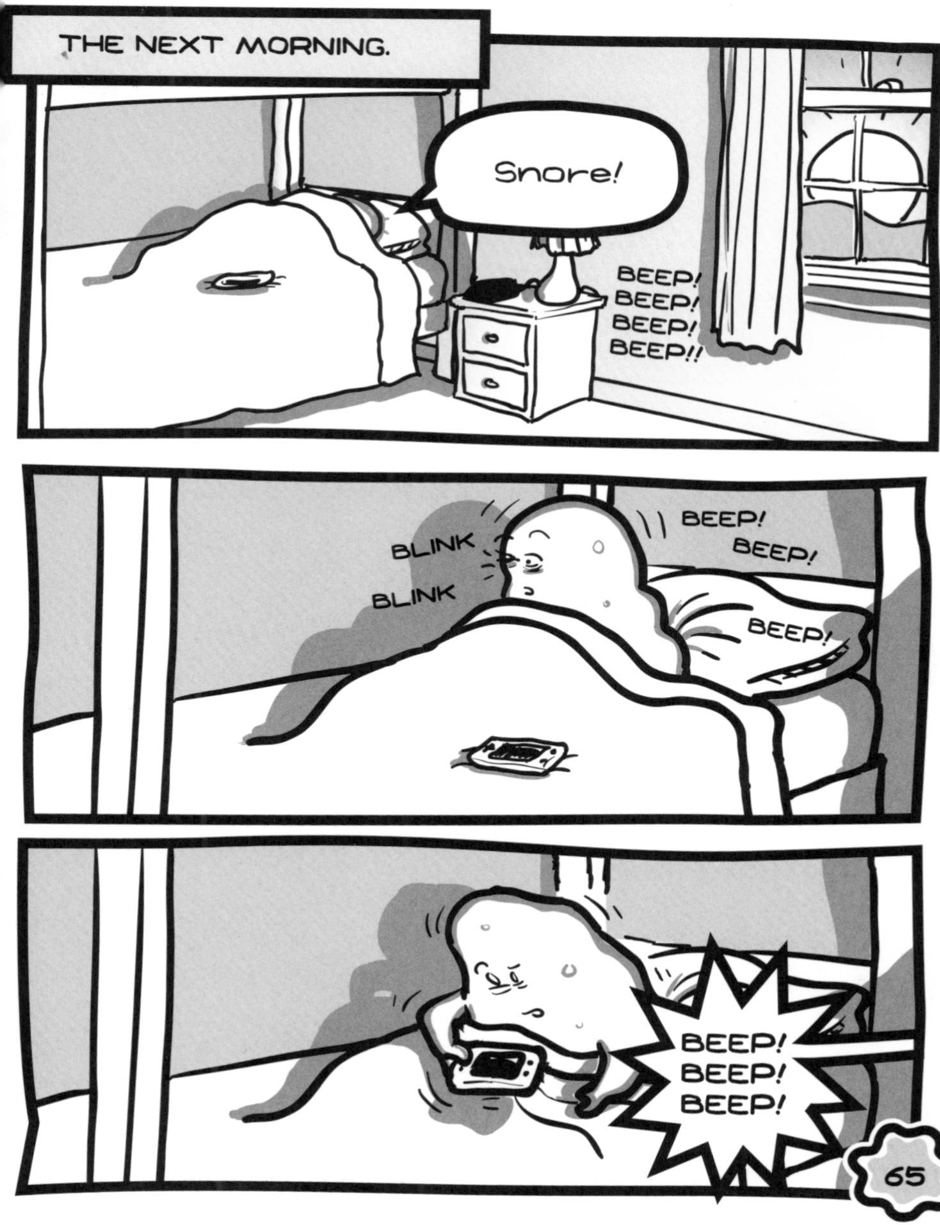
THE NEXT MORNING.
Snore!
BEEP! BEEP! BEEP! BEEP!!
BLINK
BLINK
BEEP!
BEEP!
BEEP!
BEEP! BEEP! BEEP!

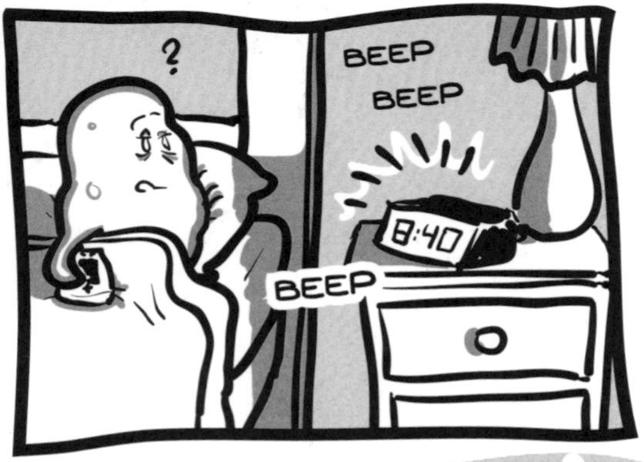
?
BEEP
BEEP
BEEP

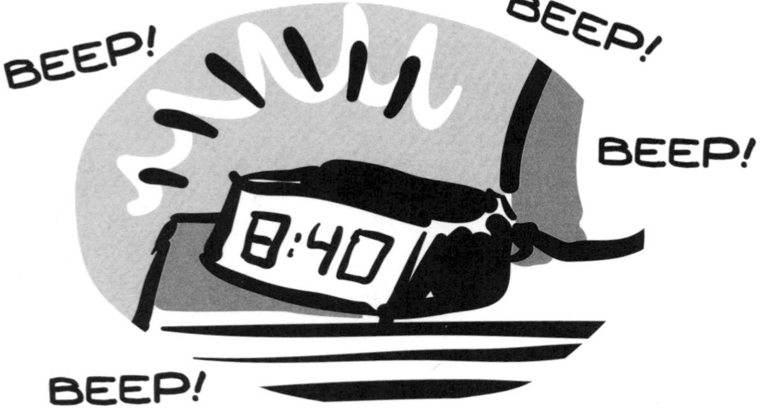
BEEP!
BEEP!
BEEP!
BEEP!

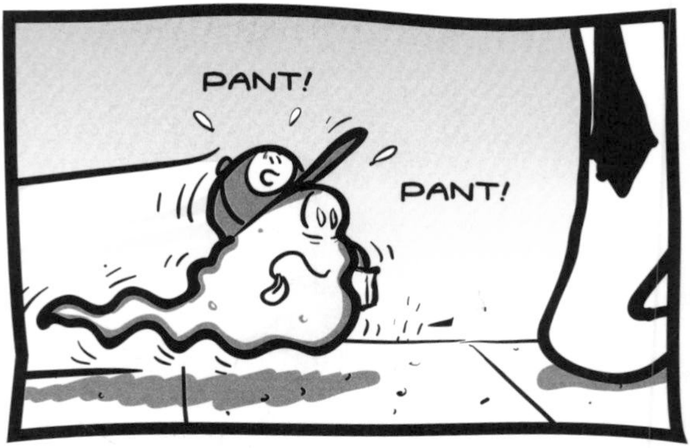
PANT!
PANT!

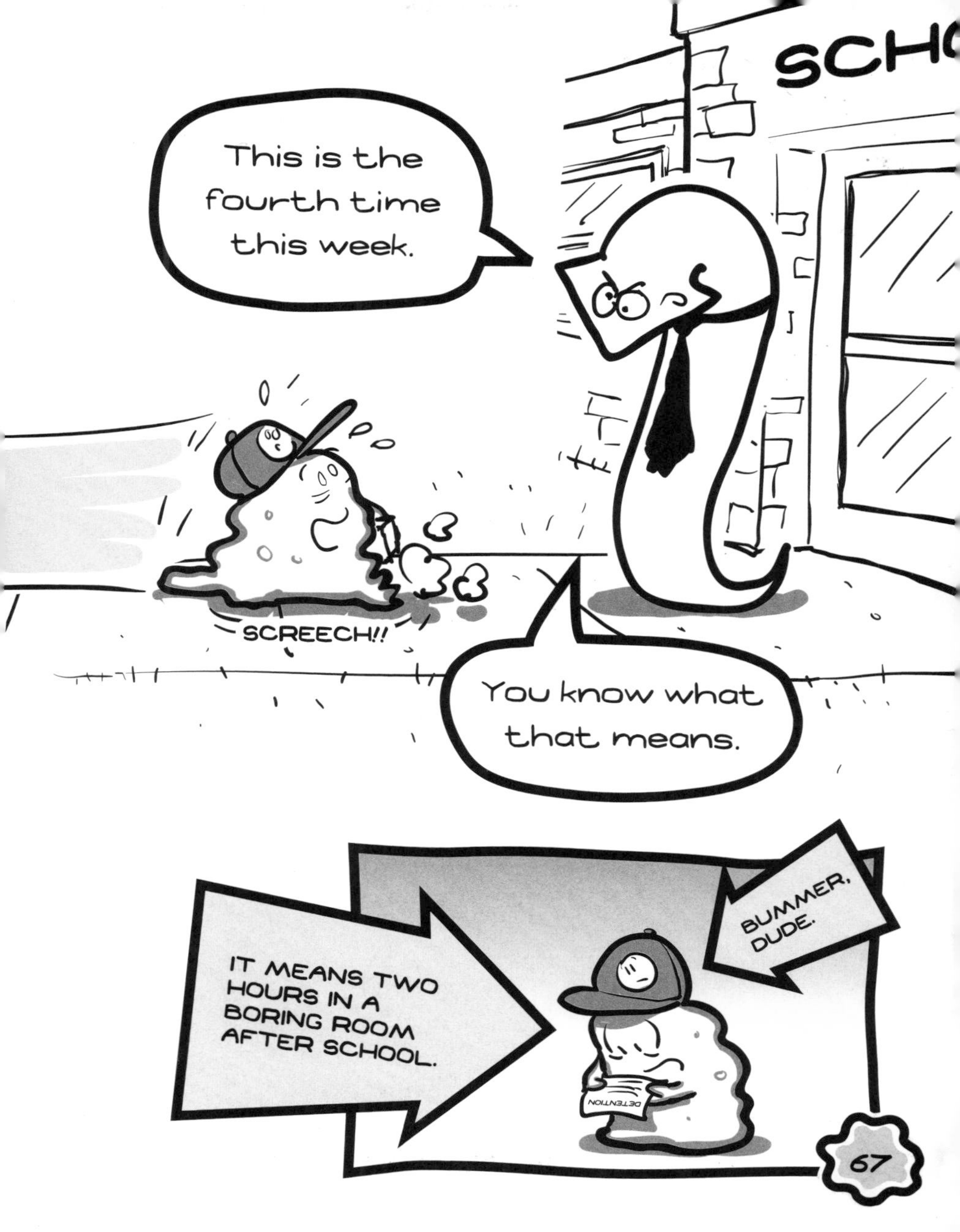

SCH
This is the fourth time this week.
SCREECH!!
You know what that means.
IT MEANS TWO HOURS IN A BORING ROOM AFTER SCHOOL.
BUMMER, DUDE.
DETENTION

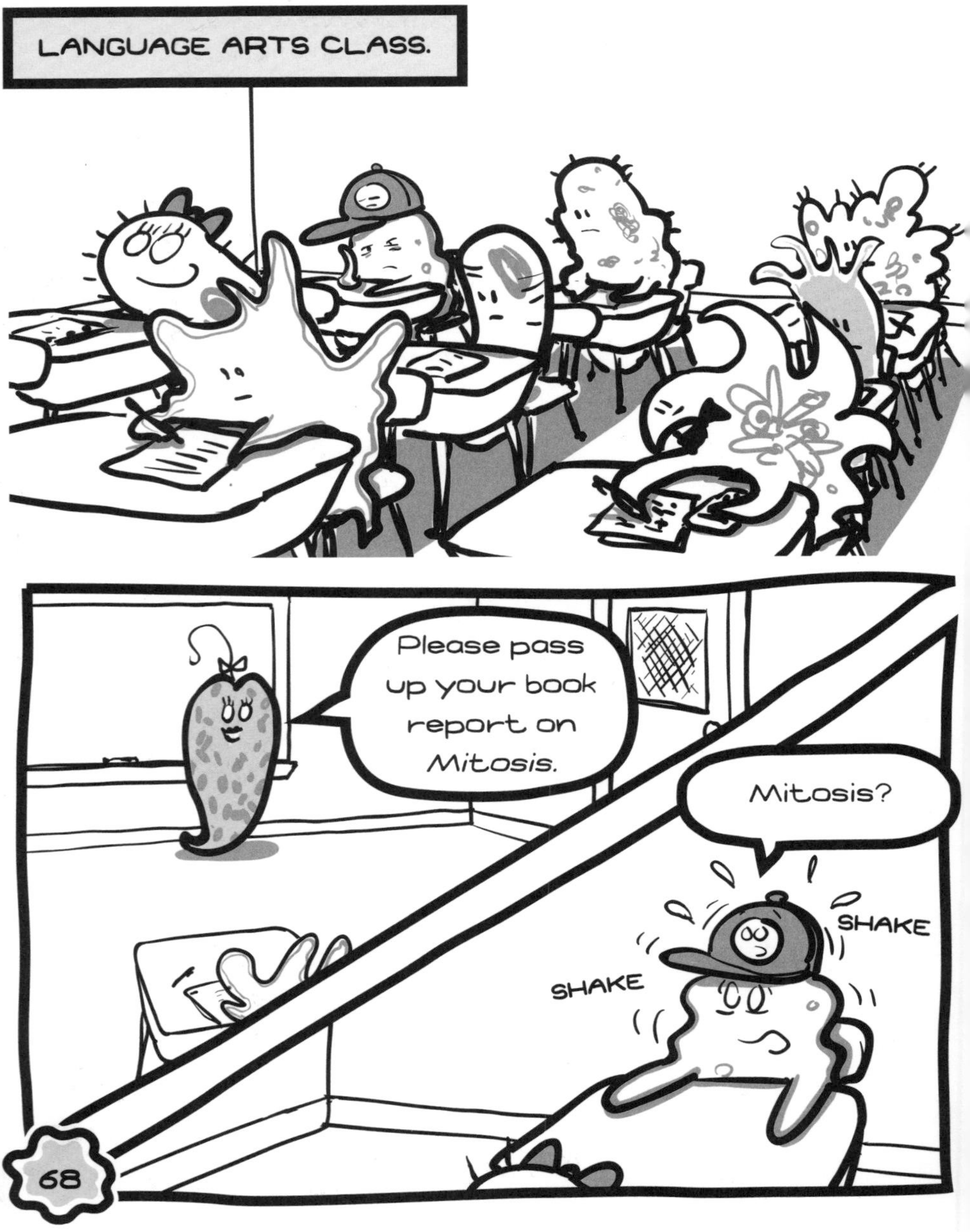
LANGUAGE ARTS CLASS.
Please pass up your book report on Mitosis.
Mitosis?
SHAKE
SHAKE

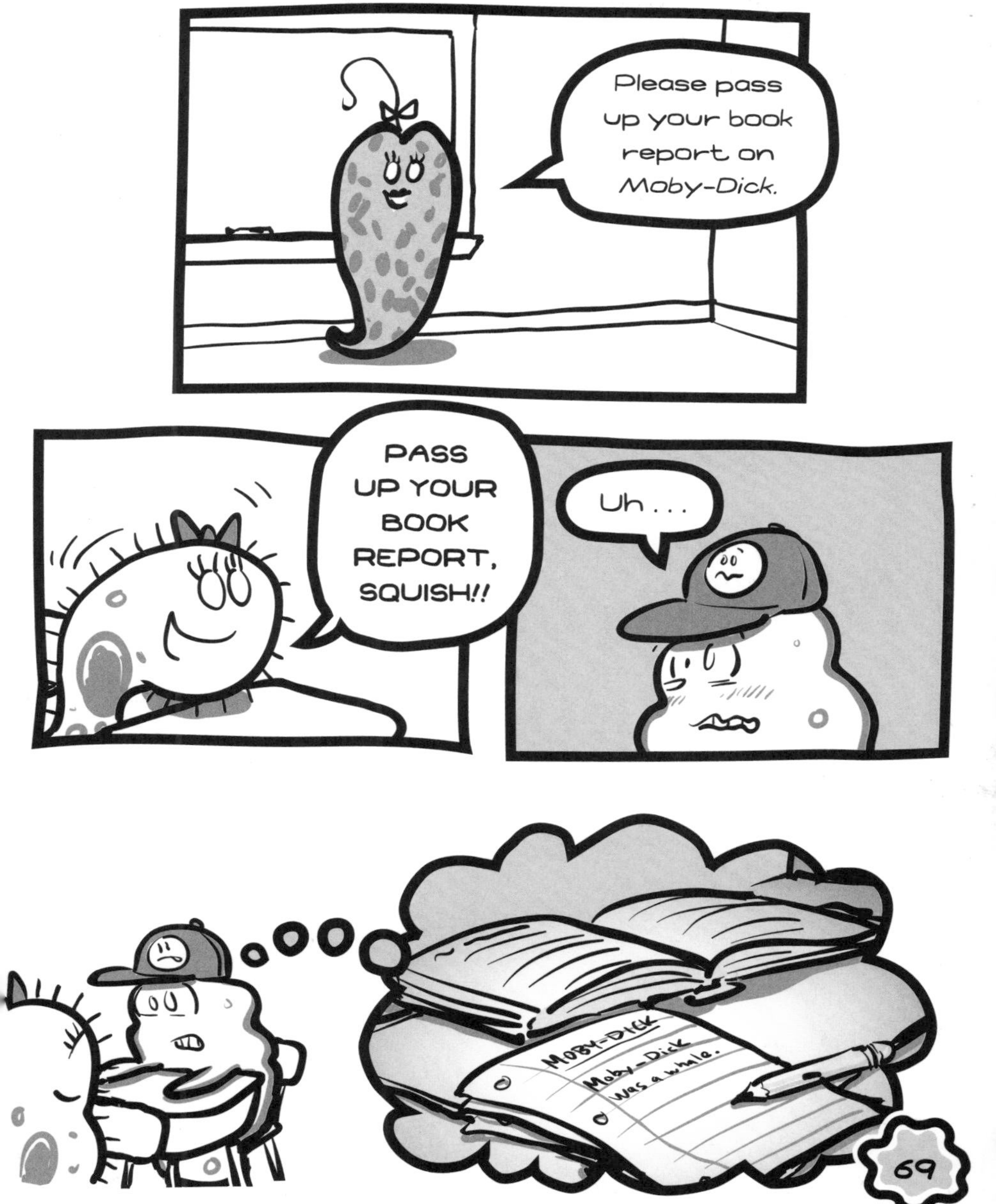

Please pass up your book report on *Moby-Dick*.
PASS UP YOUR BOOK REPORT, SQUISH!!
Uh . . .
MOBY-DICK
Moby-Dick was a whale.

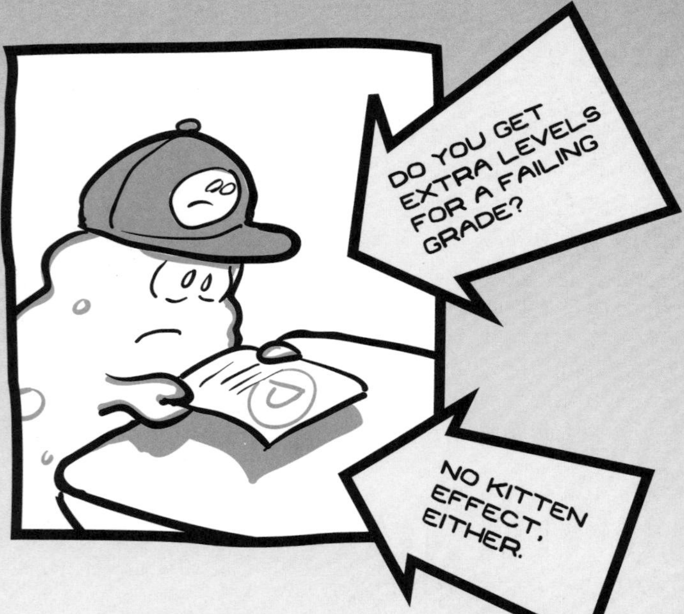
DO YOU GET EXTRA LEVELS FOR A FAILING GRADE?
NO KITTEN EFFECT, EITHER.

THAT NIGHT.

2:01

BEEP!

BEEP! BEEP!

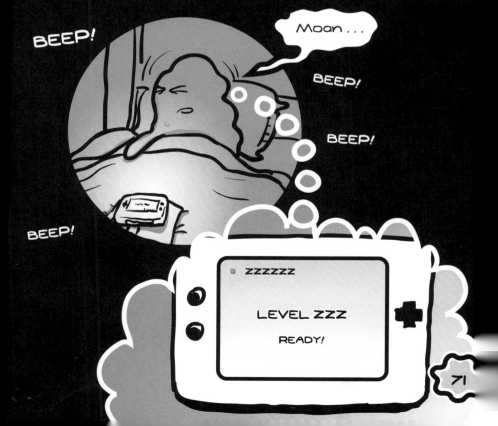

BEEP!

Moan . . .

BEEP!

BEEP!

BEEP!

ZZZZZZ

LEVEL ZZZ

READY!

71

ZZZZZZ

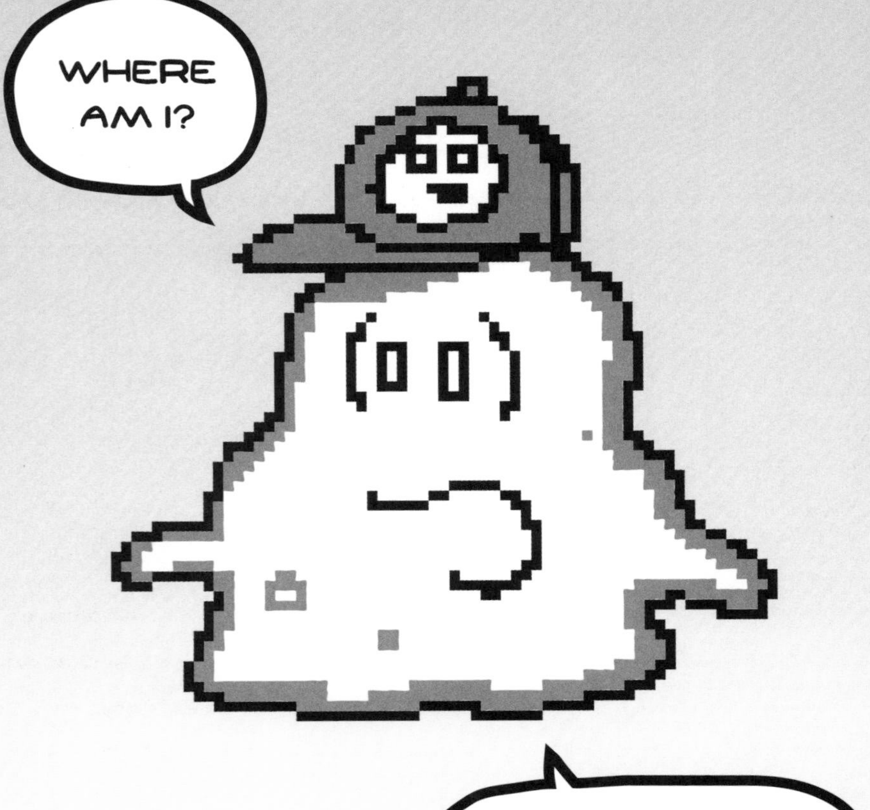
WHERE AM I?
WHY AM I PIXELATED?

LEVEL UP!

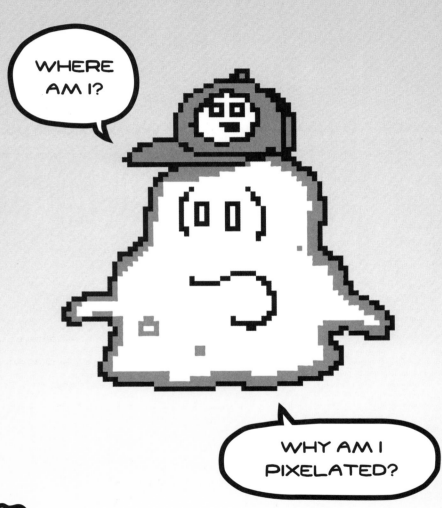

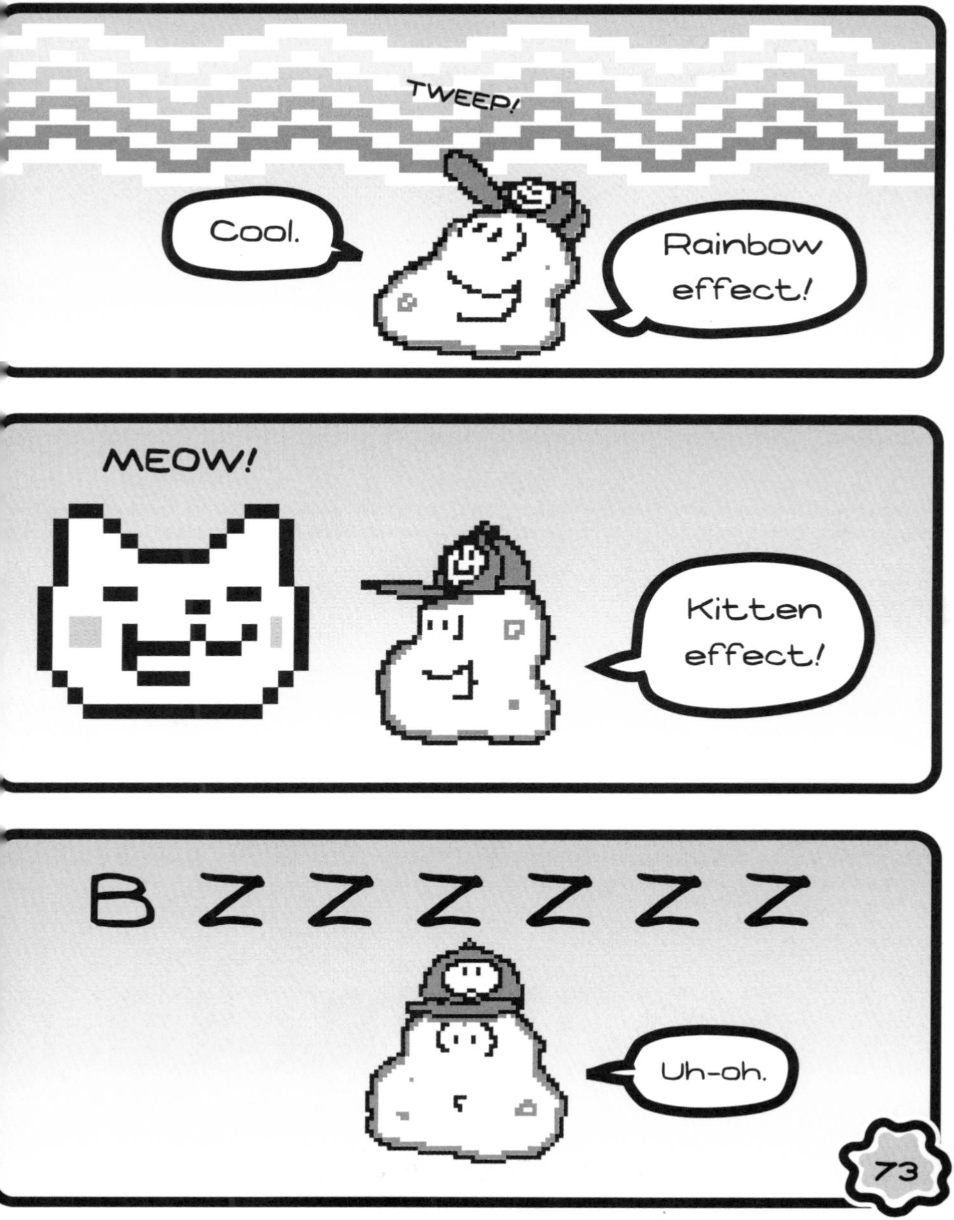
TWEEP!
Cool.
Rainbow effect!
MEOW!
Kitten effect!
BZZZZZZZ
Uh-oh.

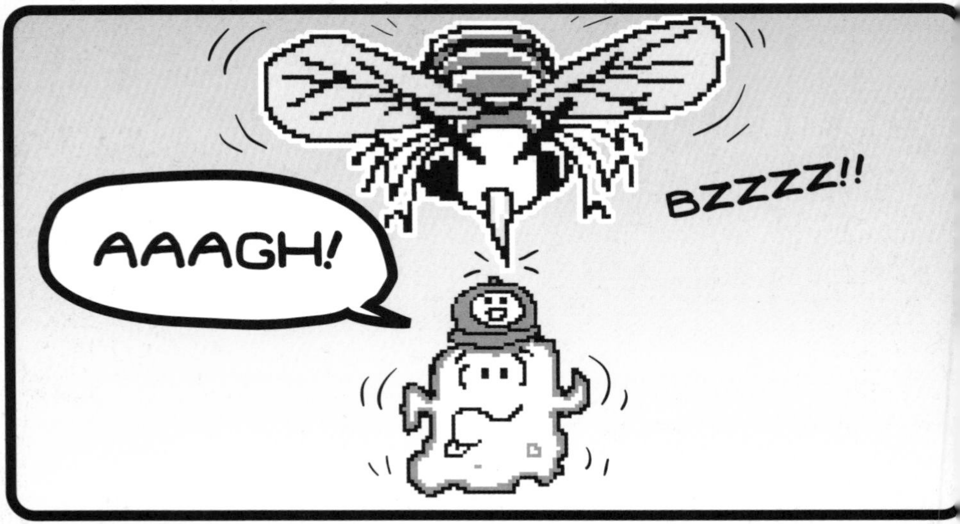
AAAGH!
BZZZZ!!

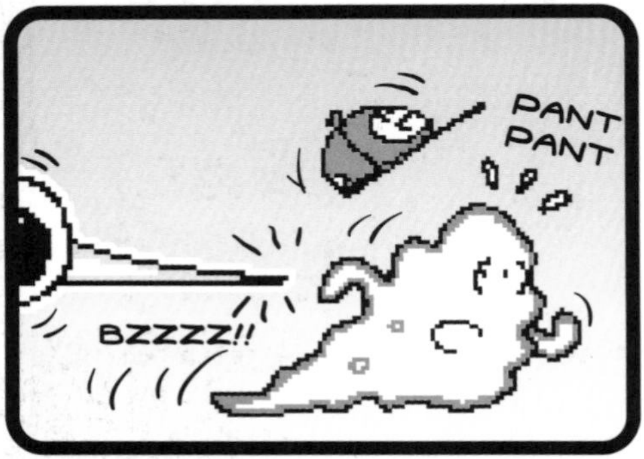
PANT
PANT
BZZZZ!!

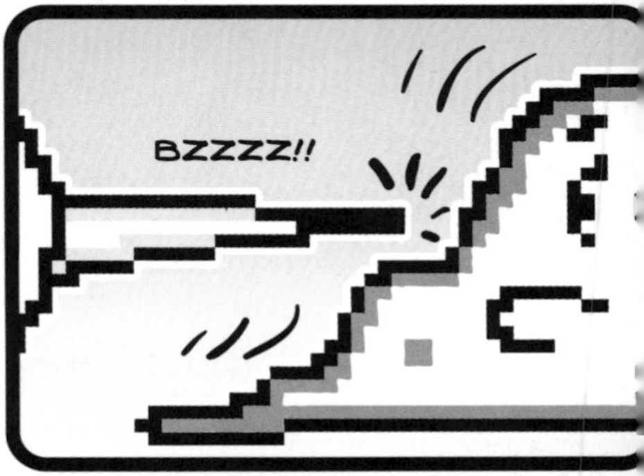
BZZZZ!!

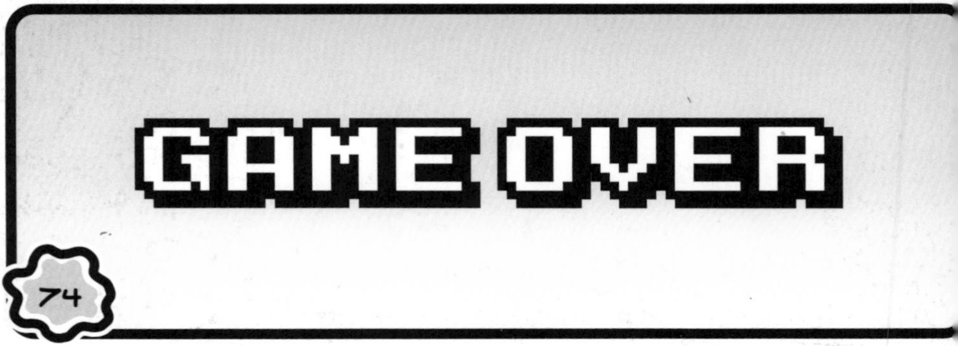
GAME OVER

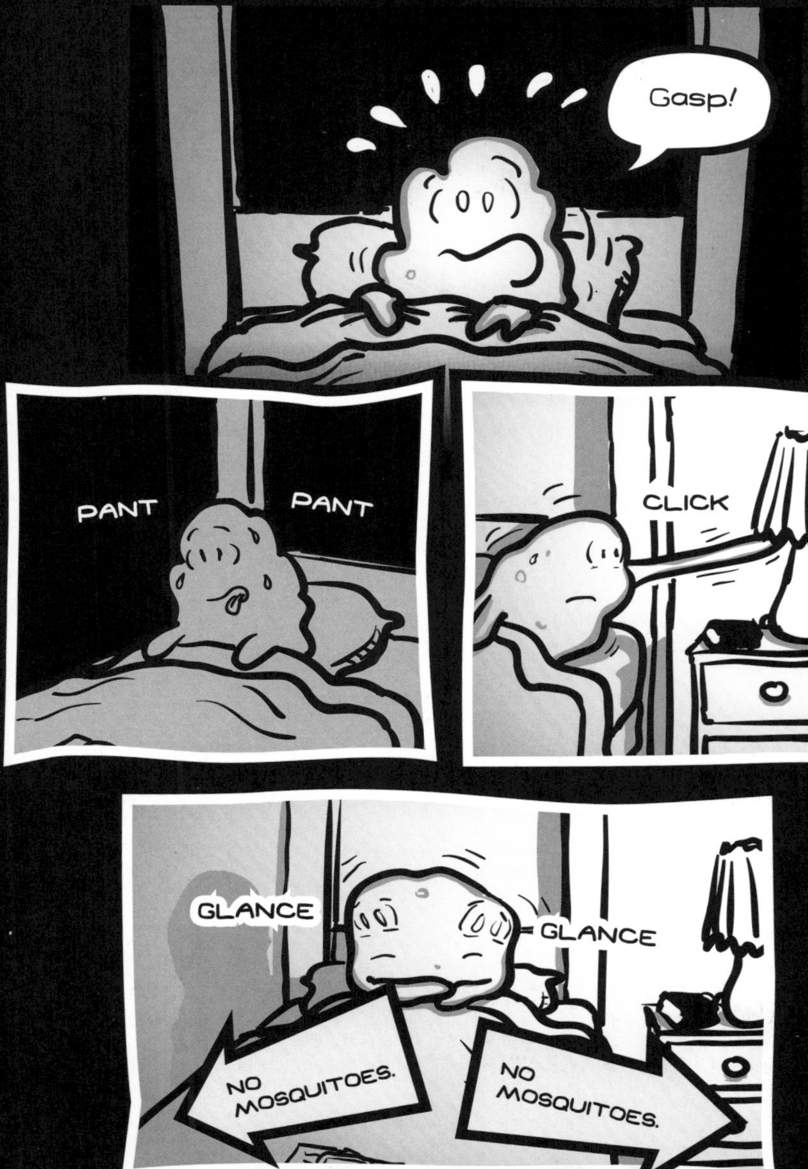
Gasp!
PANT
PANT
CLICK
GLANCE
GLANCE
NO MOSQUITOES.
NO MOSQUITOES.

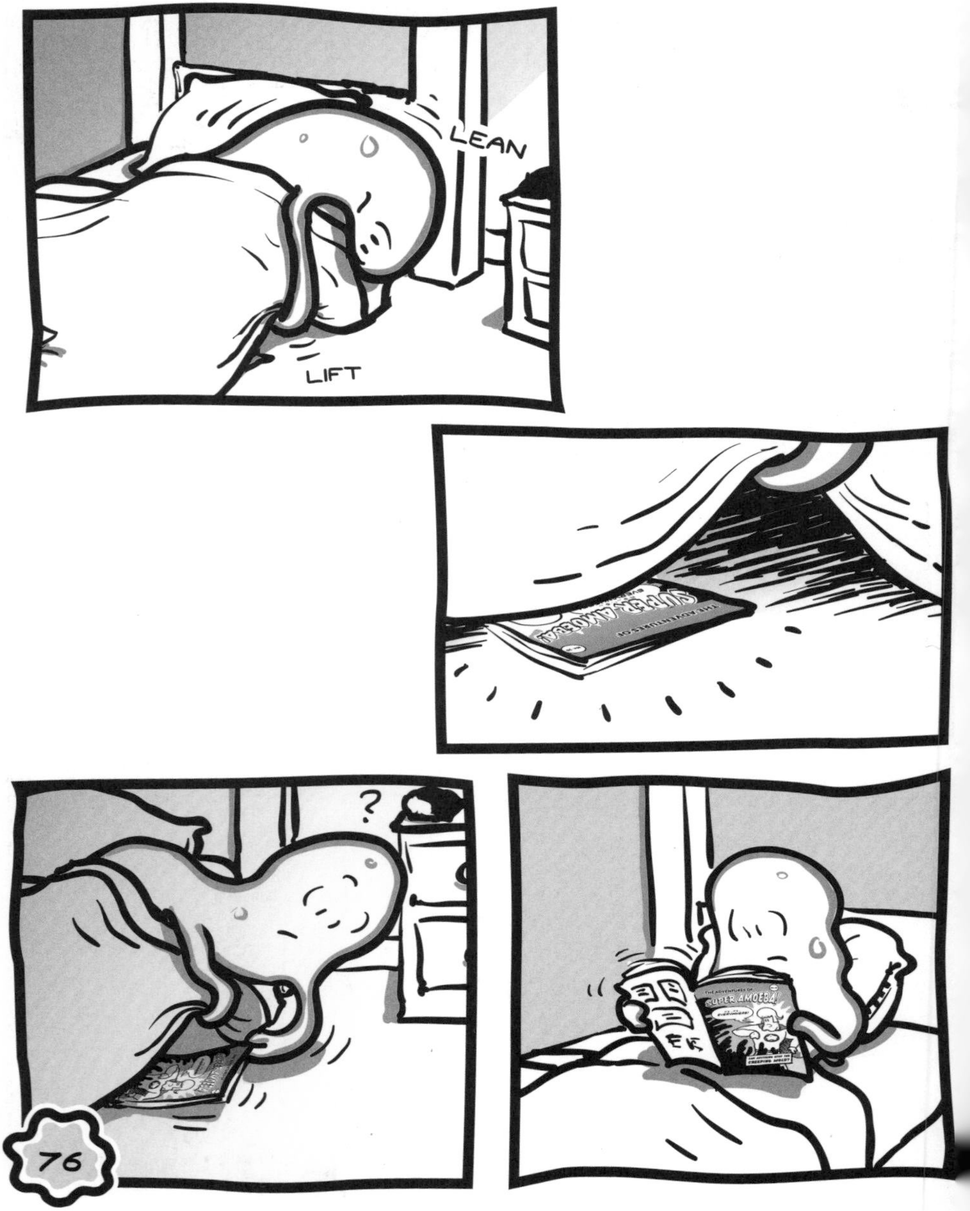
LEAN
LIFT
THE ADVENTURES OF
SUPER AMOEBA!
?
THE ADVENTURES OF
SUPER AMOEBA!

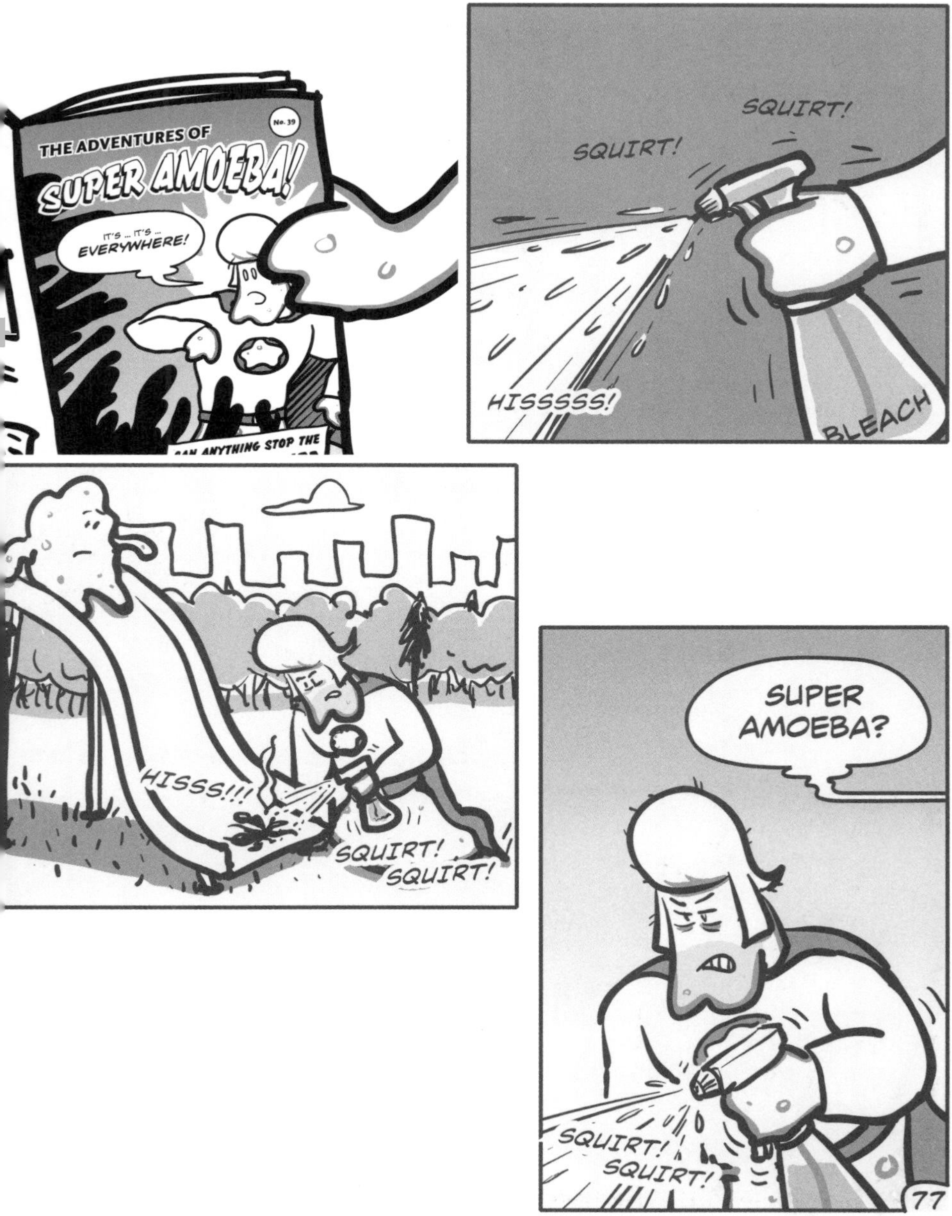
No. 39
THE ADVENTURES OF
SUPER AMOEBA!
IT'S ... IT'S ... EVERYWHERE!
ANYTHING STOP THE
SQUIRT!
SQUIRT!
HISSSSS!
BLEACH
HISSS!!!
SQUIRT!
SQUIRT!
SUPER AMOEBA?
SQUIRT!
SQUIRT!

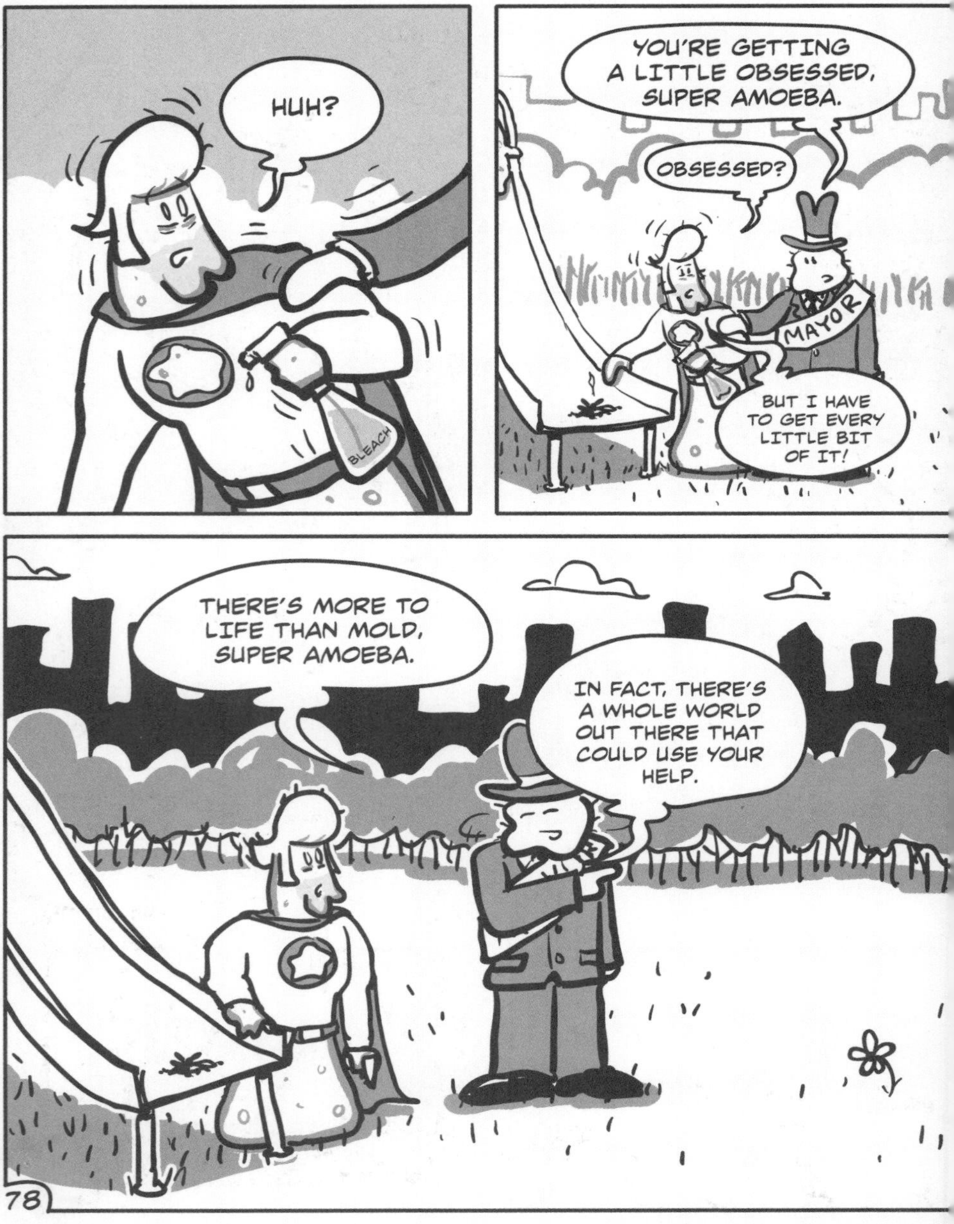
HUH?
BLEACH
YOU'RE GETTING A LITTLE OBSESSED, SUPER AMOEBA.
OBSESSED?
MAYOR
BUT I HAVE TO GET EVERY LITTLE BIT OF IT!
THERE'S MORE TO LIFE THAN MOLD, SUPER AMOEBA.
IN FACT, THERE'S A WHOLE WORLD OUT THERE THAT COULD USE YOUR HELP.

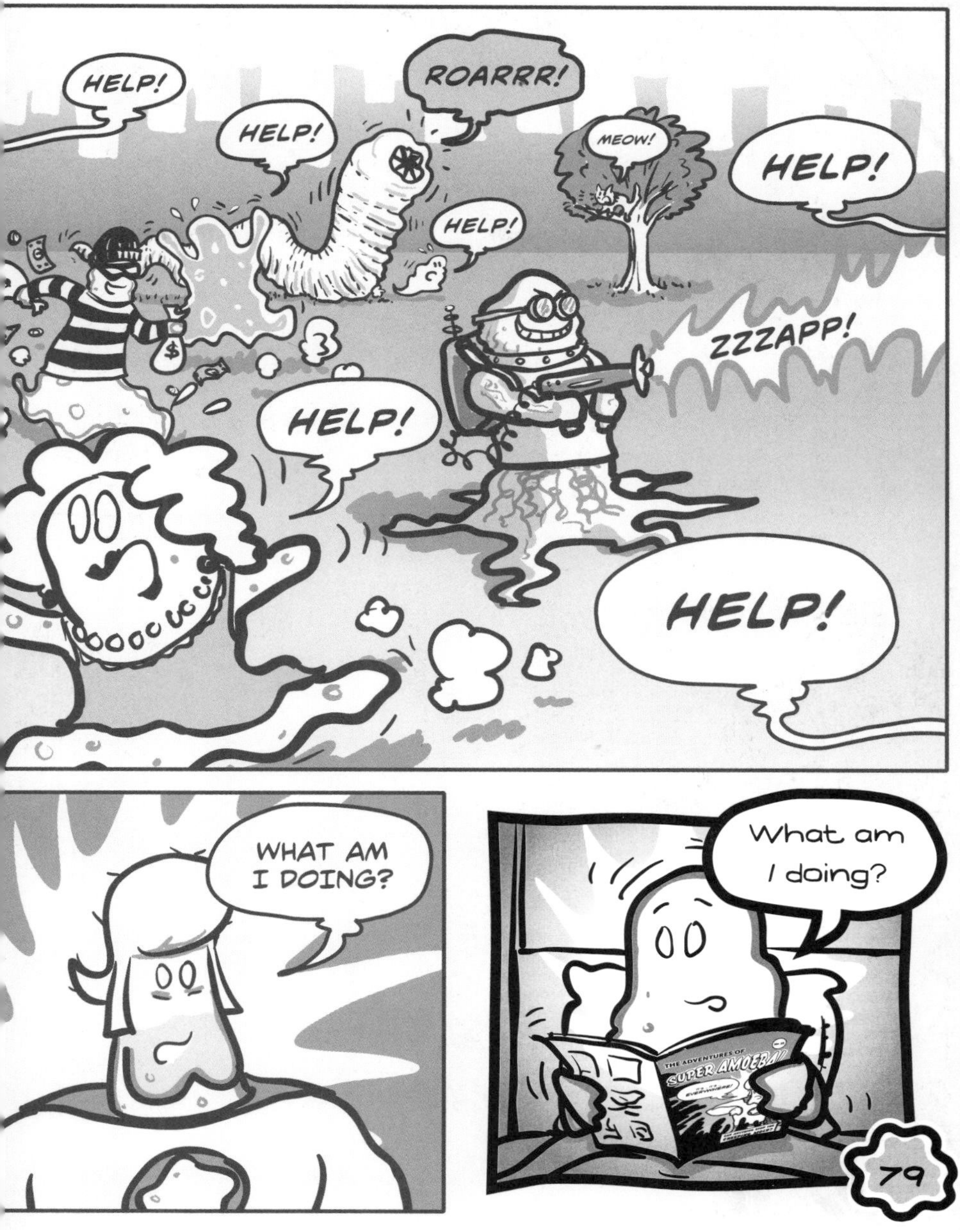
HELP!
HELP!
ROARRR!
HELP!
MEOW!
HELP!
ZZZAPP!
HELP!
HELP!
WHAT AM I DOING?
What am I doing?
THE ADVENTURES OF
SUPER AMOEBA!

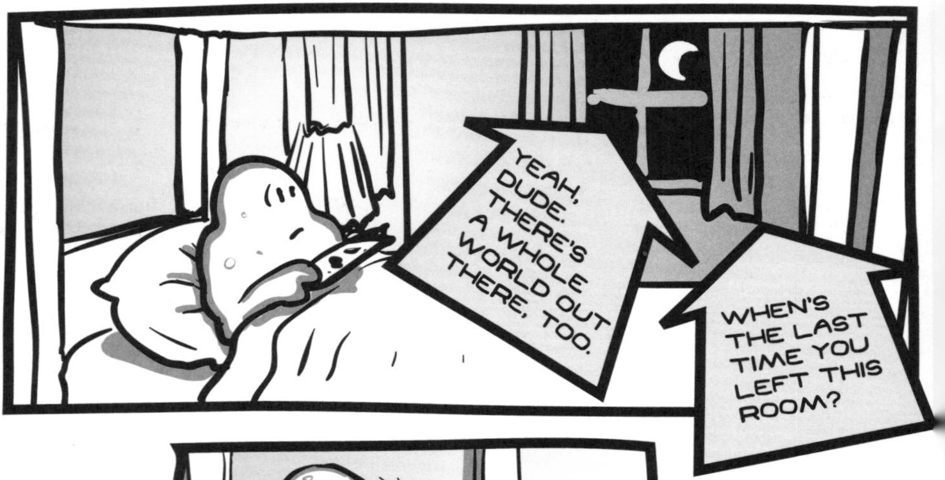
YEAH, DUDE. THERE'S A WHOLE WORLD OUT THERE, TOO.
WHEN'S THE LAST TIME YOU LEFT THIS ROOM?

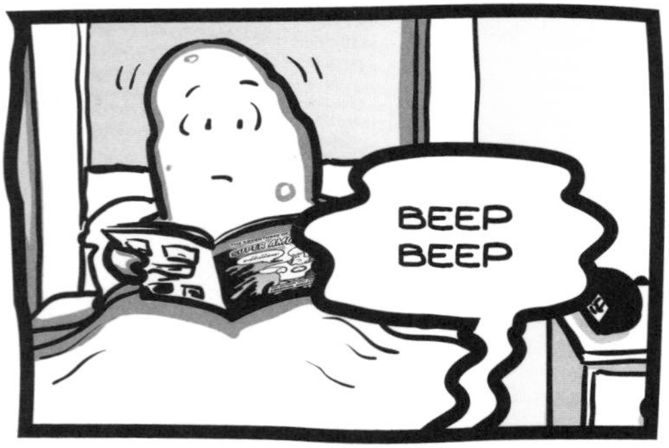
BEEP BEEP

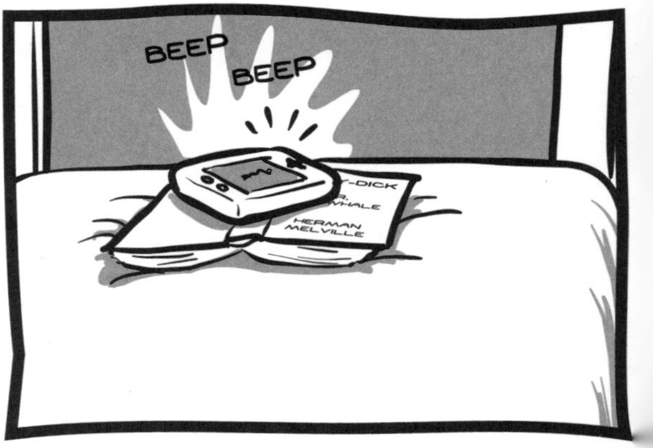
BEEP
BEEP
HERMAN MELVILLE

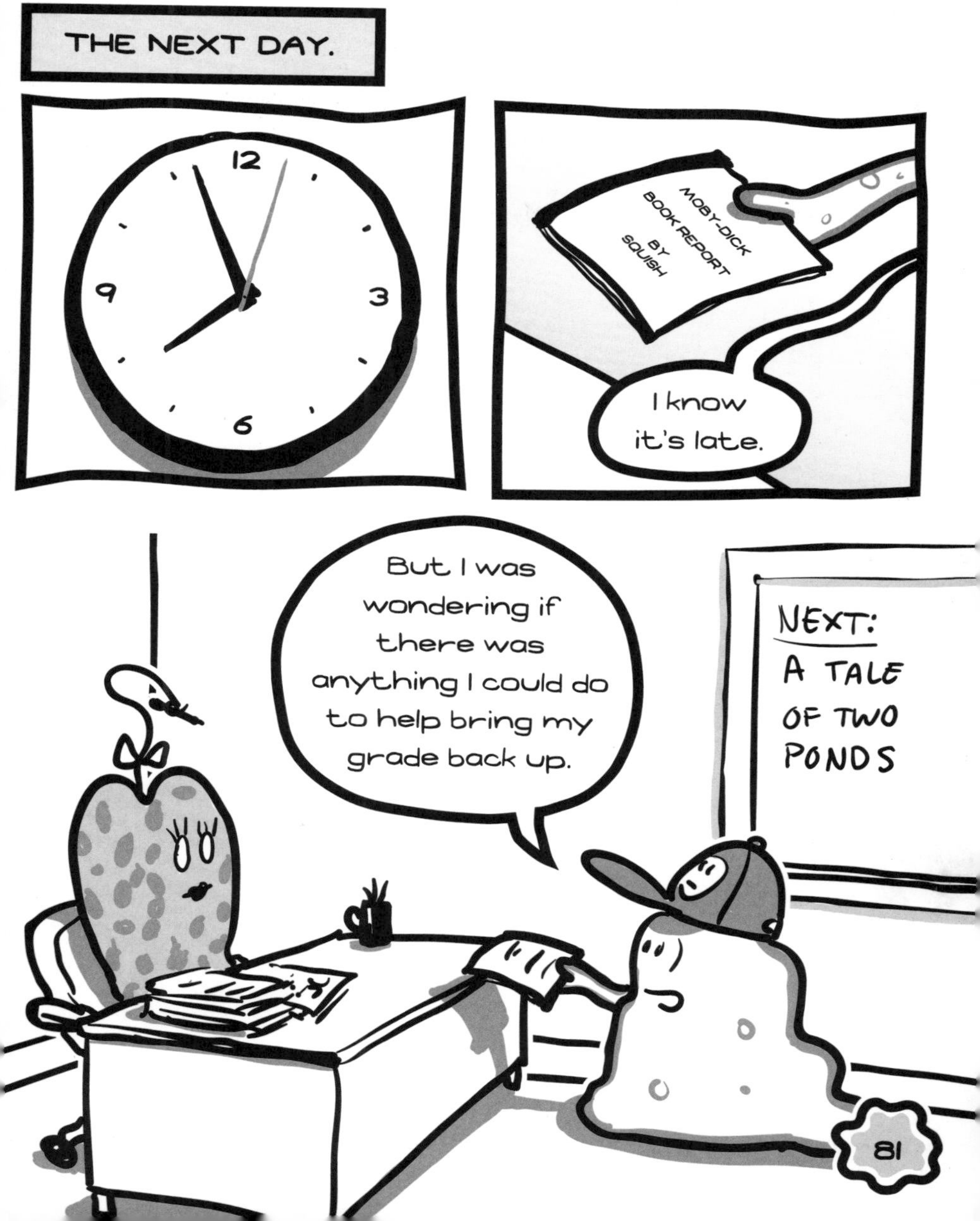
THE NEXT DAY.
MOBY-DICK BOOK REPORT BY SQUISH
I know it's late.
But I was wondering if there was anything I could do to help bring my grade back up.
NEXT: A TALE OF TWO PONDS

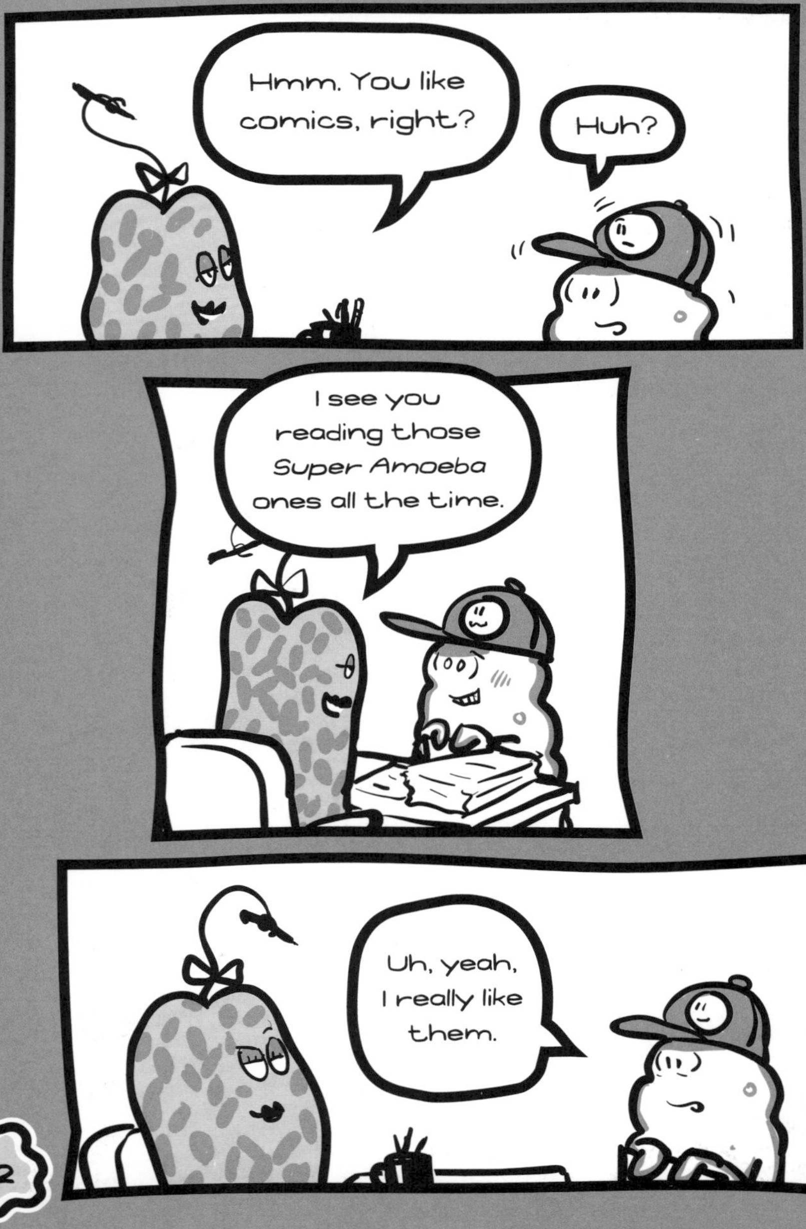
Hmm. You like comics, right?
Huh?
I see you reading those *Super Amoeba* ones all the time.
Uh, yeah, I really like them.

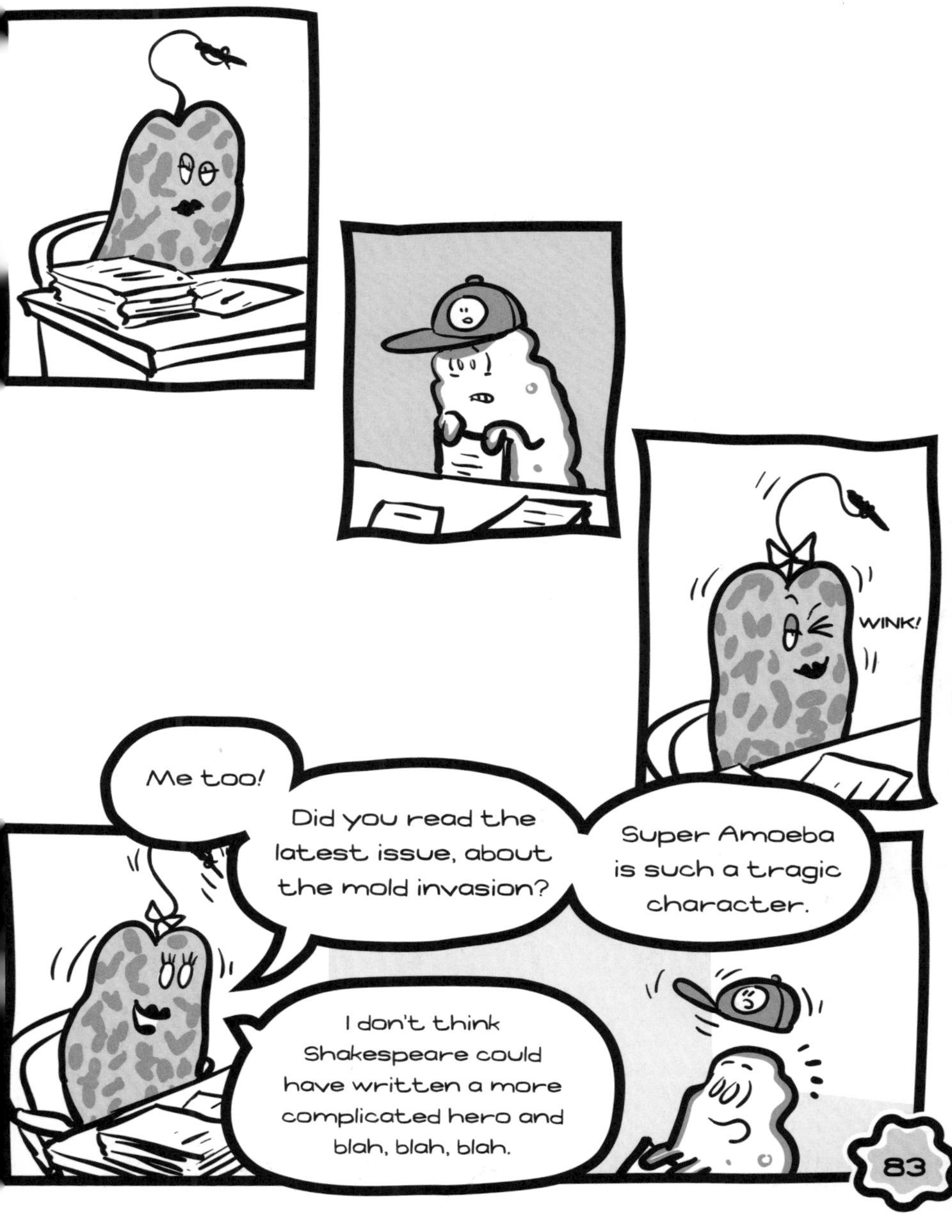
WINK!
Me too!
Did you read the latest issue, about the mold invasion?
Super Amoeba is such a tragic character.
I don't think Shakespeare could have written a more complicated hero and blah, blah, blah.

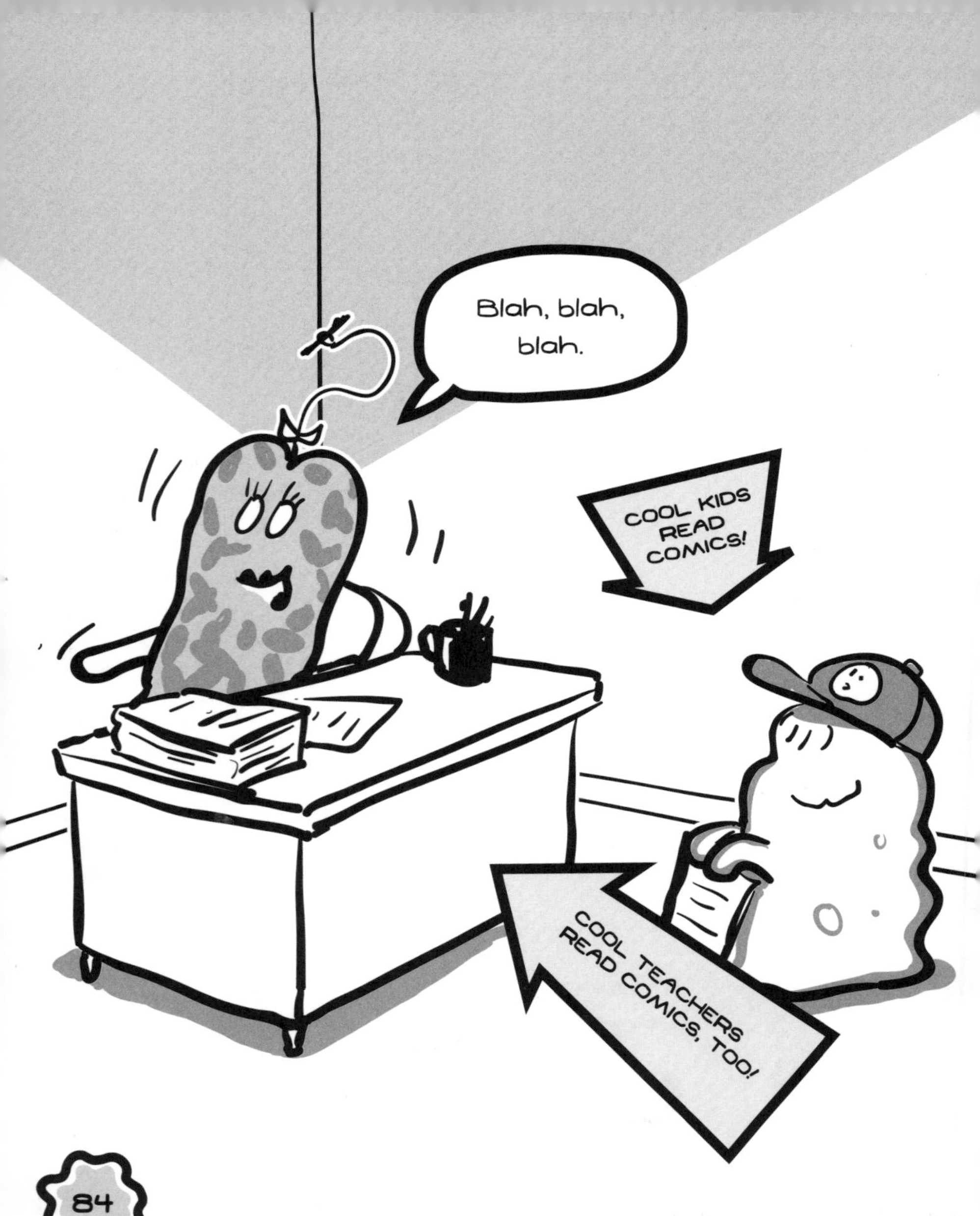
Blah, blah, blah.
COOL KIDS READ COMICS!
COOL TEACHERS READ COMICS, TOO!

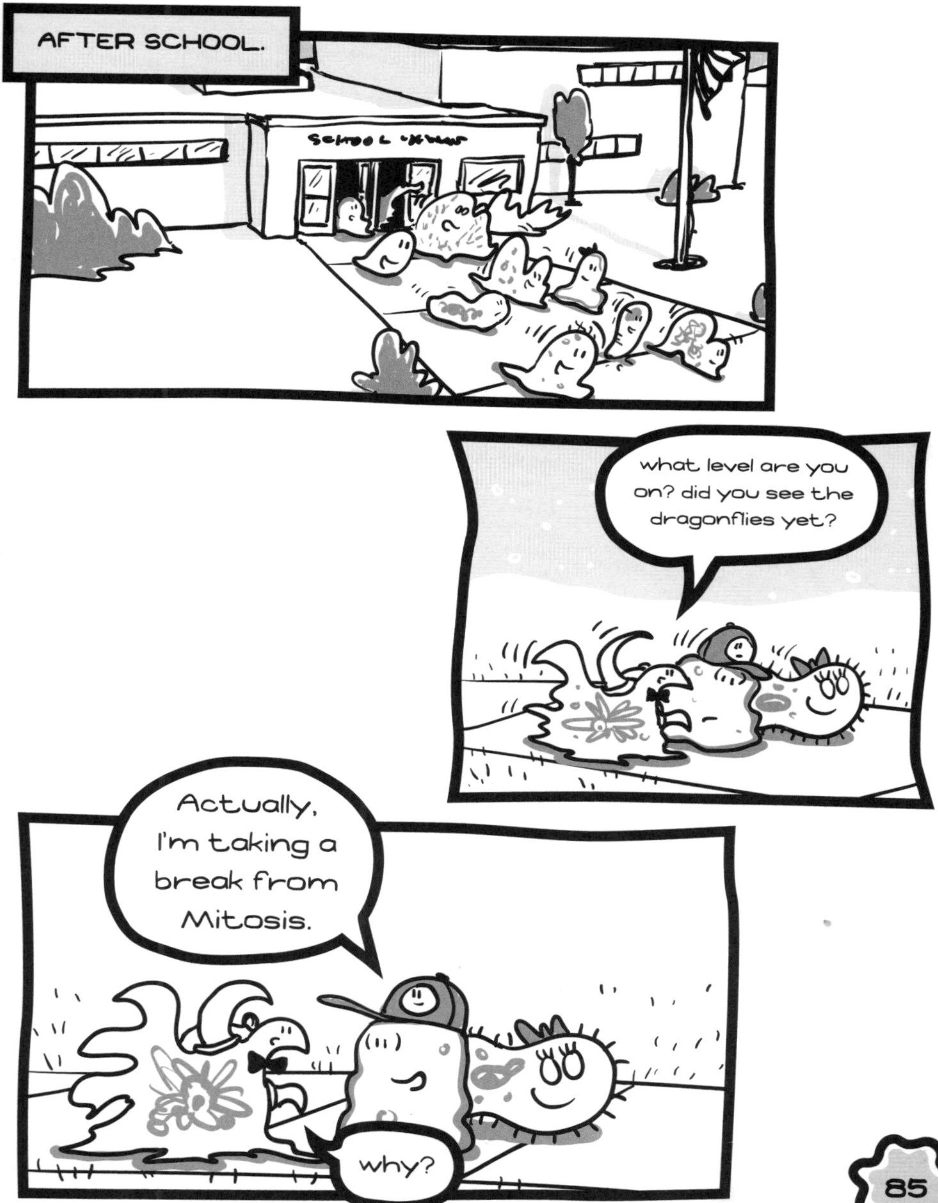
AFTER SCHOOL.
what level are you on? did you see the dragonflies yet?
Actually, I'm taking a break from Mitosis.
why?

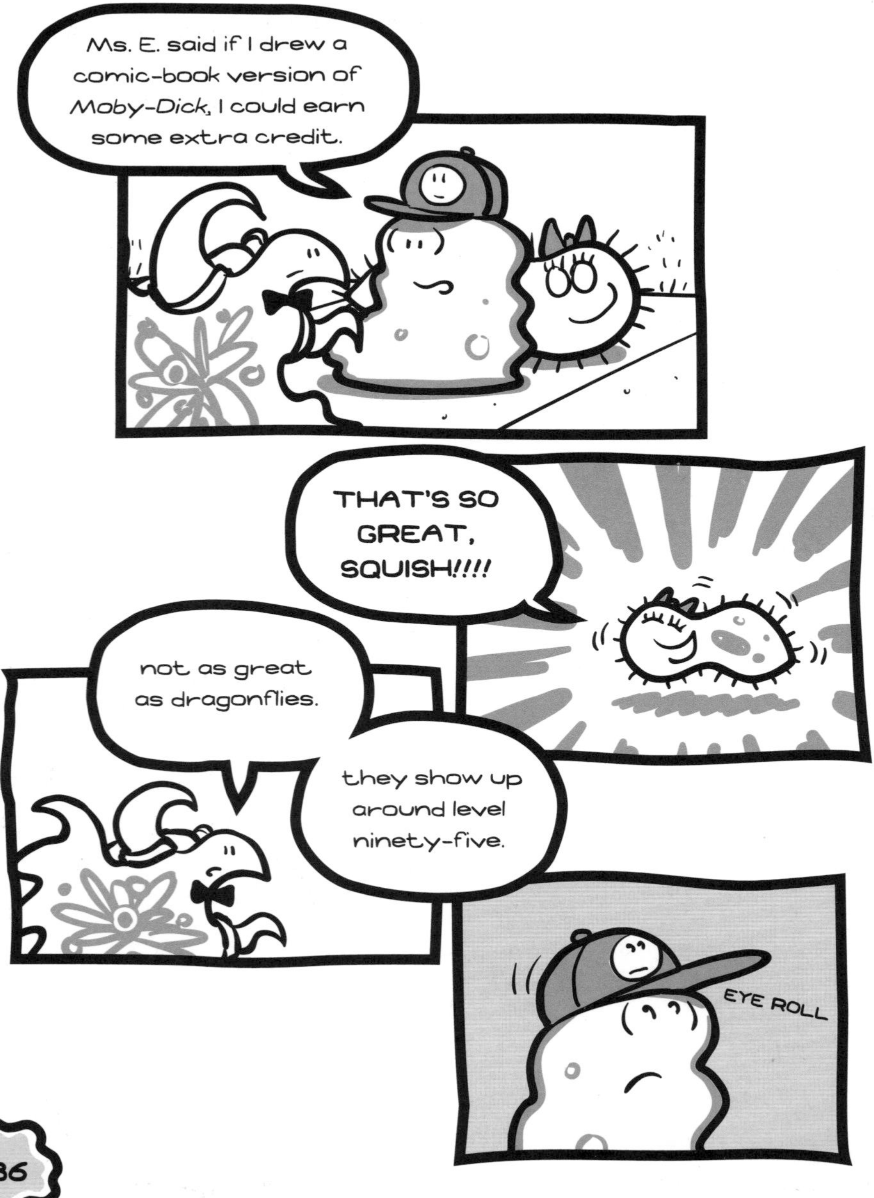
Ms. E. said if I drew a comic-book version of *Moby-Dick*, I could earn some extra credit.
THAT'S SO GREAT, SQUISH!!!!!
not as great as dragonflies.
they show up around level ninety-five.
EYE ROLL

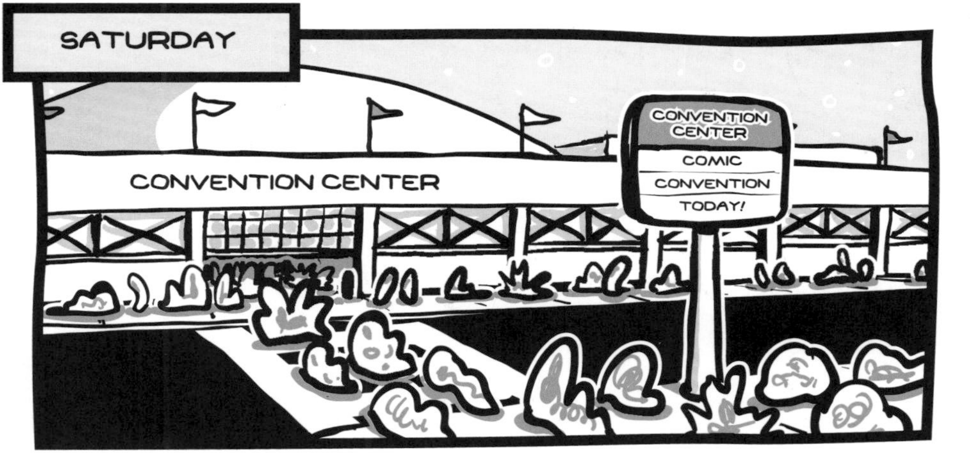
SATURDAY
CONVENTION CENTER
CONVENTION CENTER
COMIC
CONVENTION
TODAY!

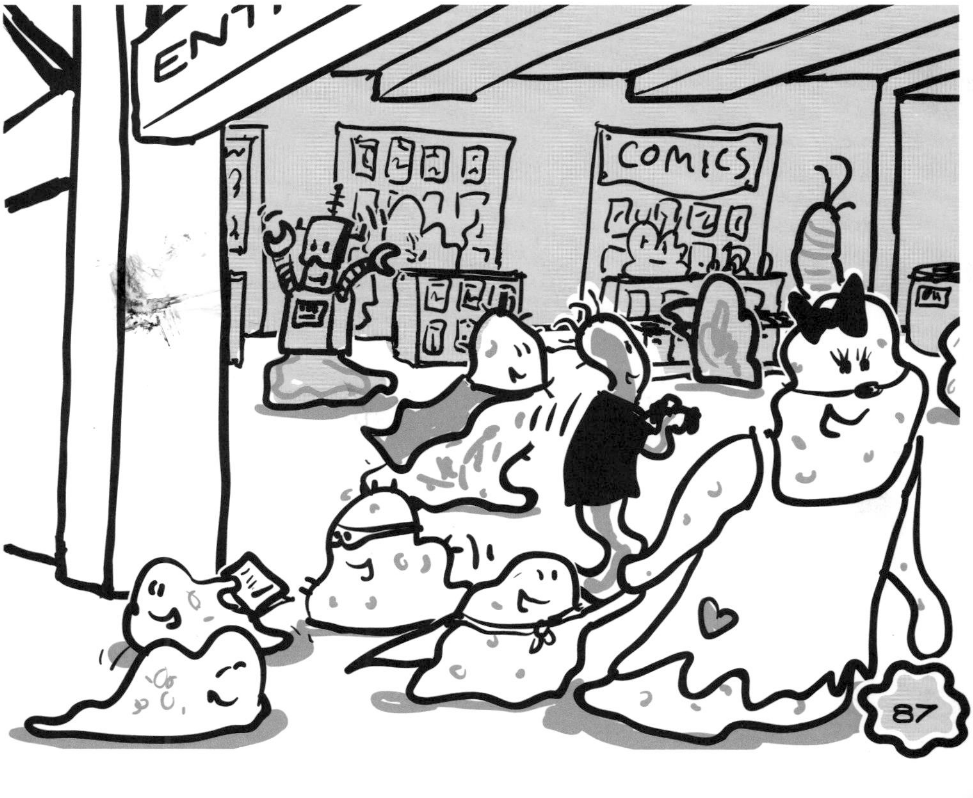
COMICS

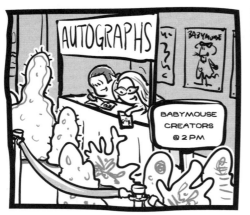

AUTOGRAPHS

BABYMOUSE

BABYMOUSE
CREATORS
@ 2 PM

MYSTERIOUS
GALAXY!

GAME
OF
CELLS

CLICK!

AUTOGRAPHS

Wow! Great
costumes! Can I take
your picture?

Sure.

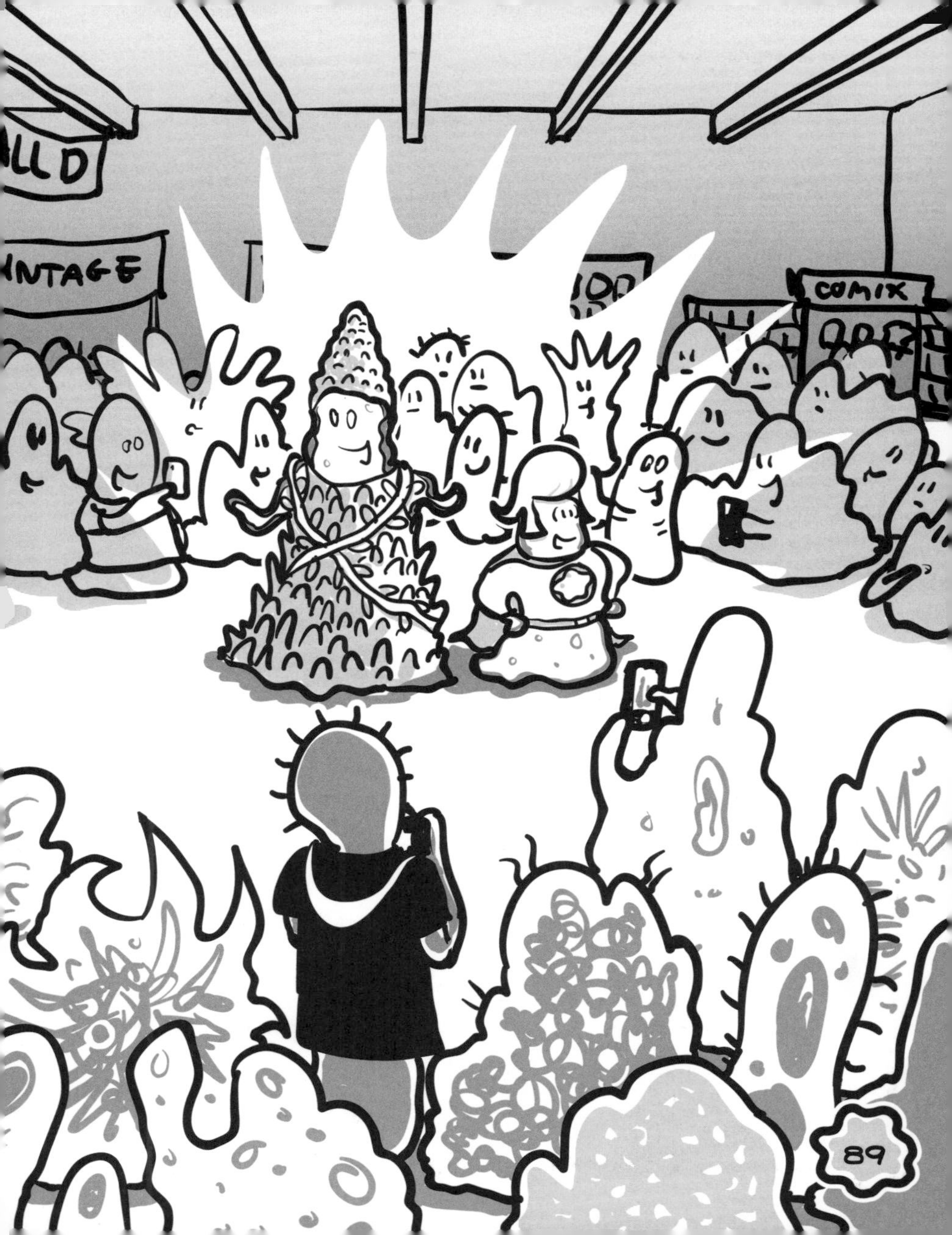
COMIX

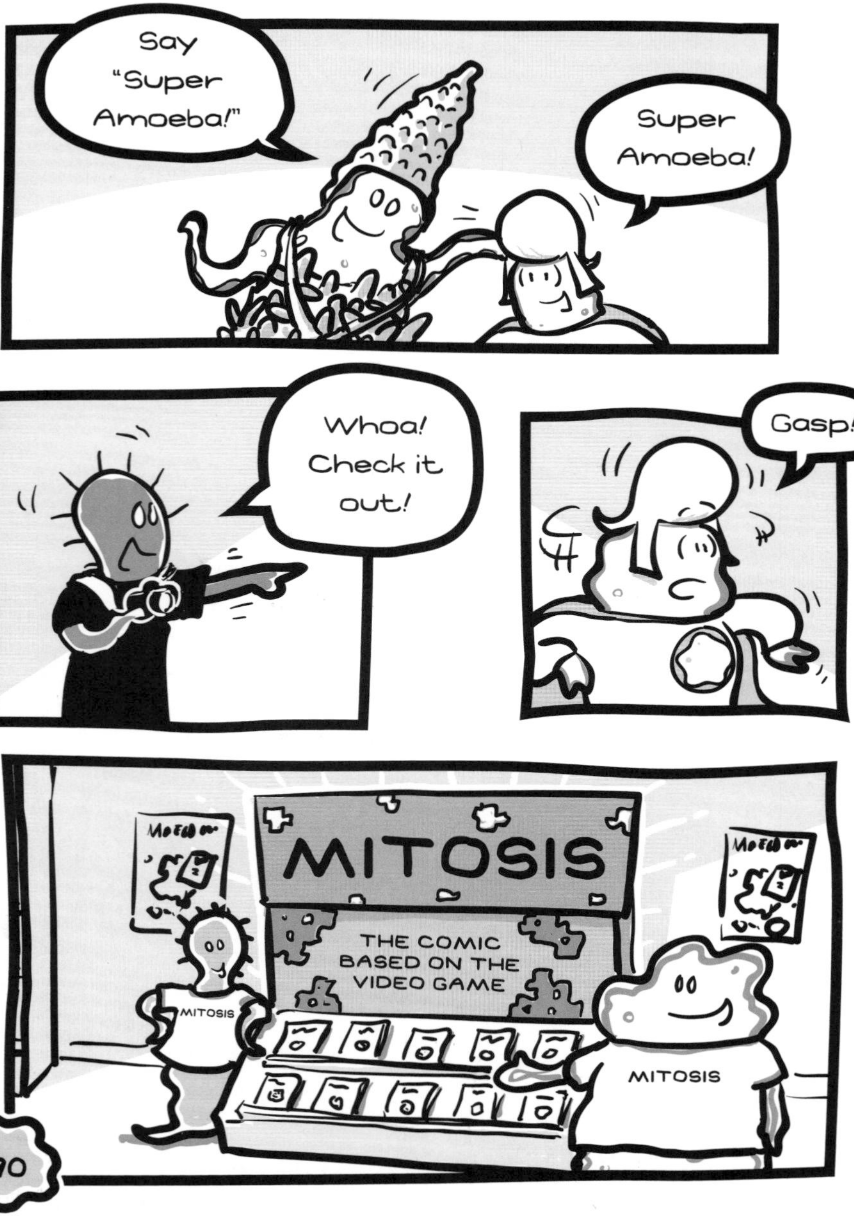
Say "Super Amoeba!"
Super Amoeba!
Whoa! Check it out!
Gasp!
MITOSIS
THE COMIC BASED ON THE VIDEO GAME
MITOSIS
MITOSIS

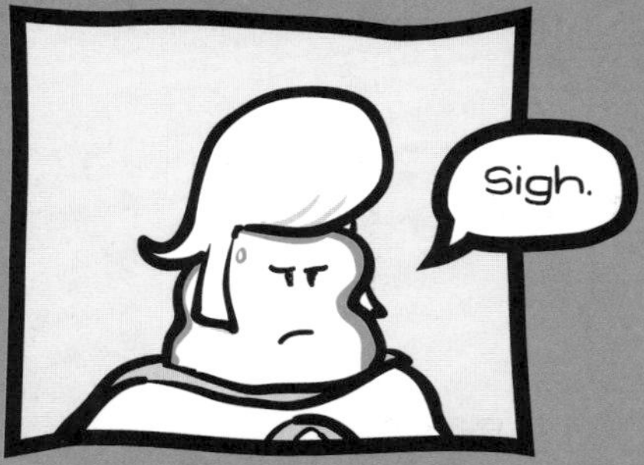
Sigh.

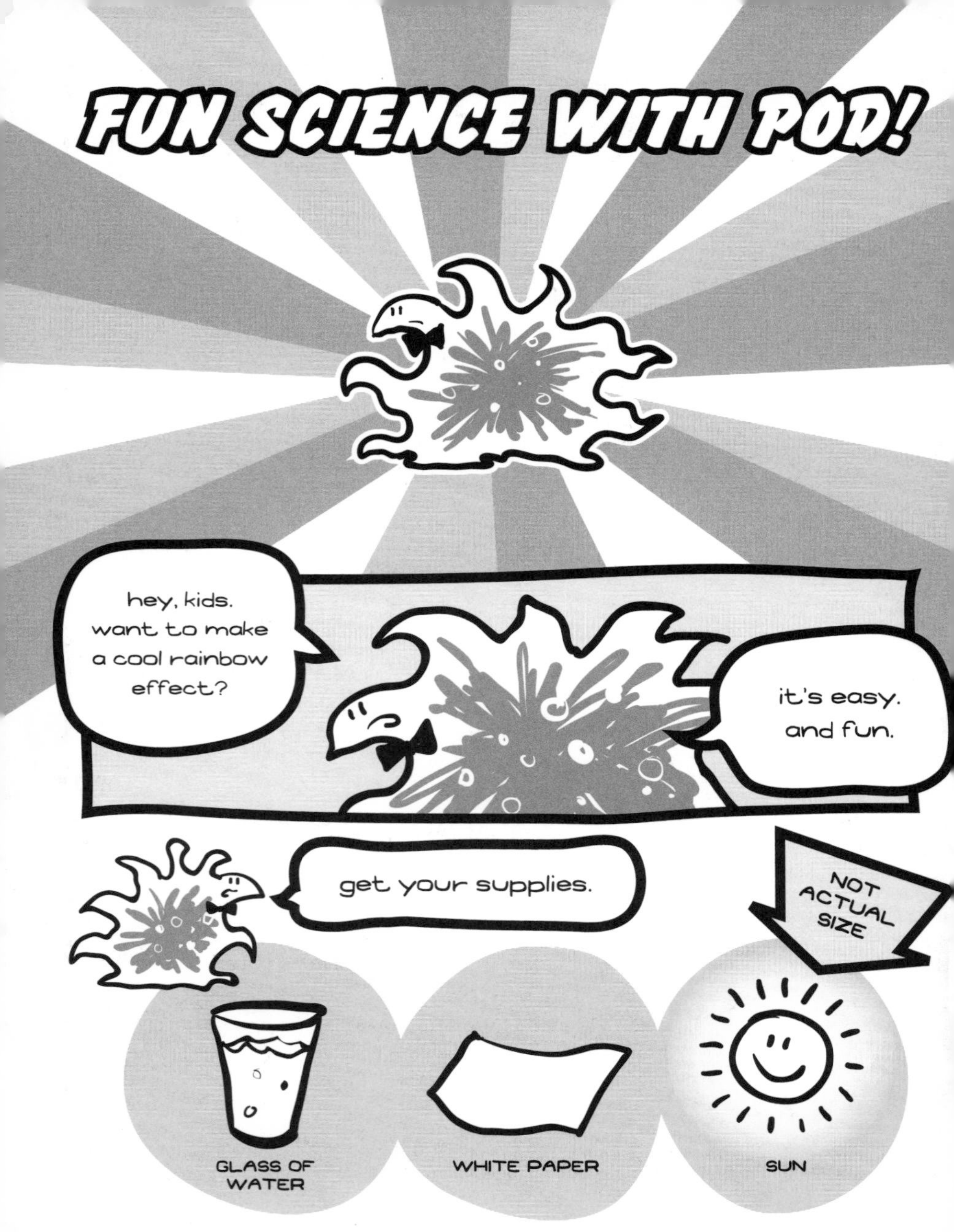
FUN SCIENCE WITH POD!
hey, kids. want to make a cool rainbow effect?
it's easy. and fun.
get your supplies.
NOT ACTUAL SIZE
GLASS OF WATER
WHITE PAPER
SUN

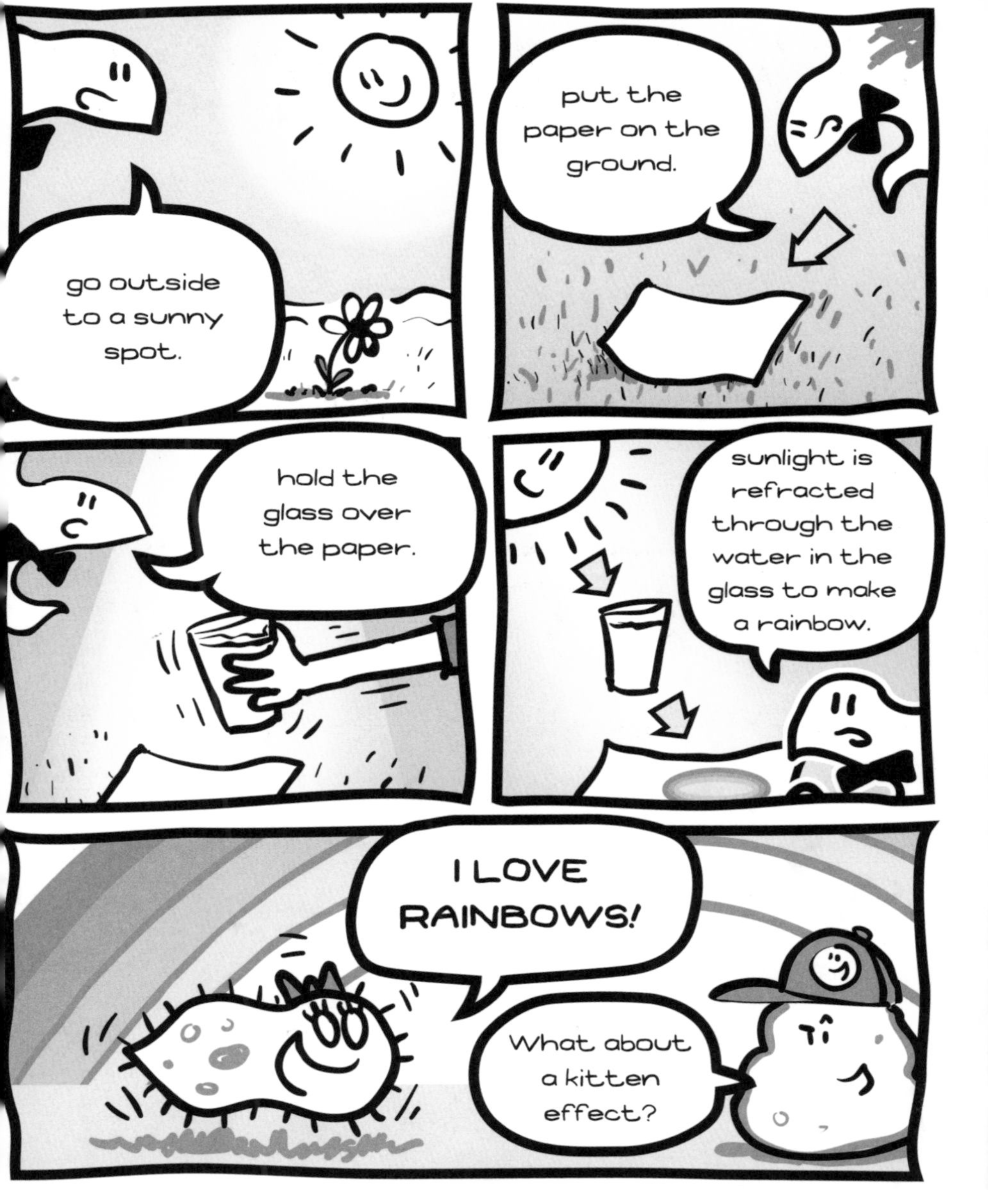
go outside to a sunny spot.
put the paper on the ground.
hold the glass over the paper.
sunlight is refracted through the water in the glass to make a rainbow.
I LOVE RAINBOWS!
What about a kitten effect?

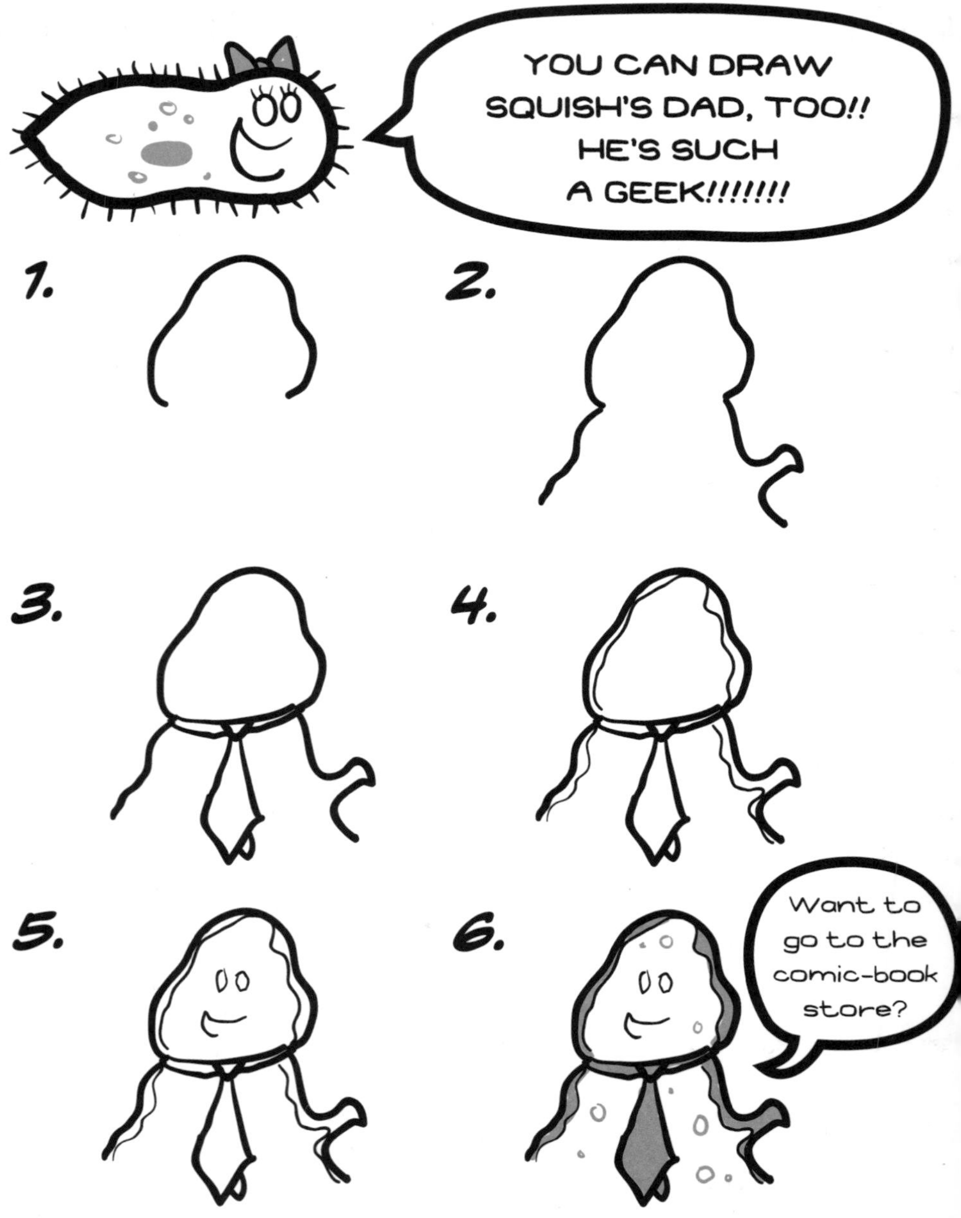
YOU CAN DRAW SQUISH'S DAD, TOO!! HE'S SUCH A GEEK!!!!!!!!
1.
2.
3.
4.
5.
6.
Want to go to the comic-book store?

IF YOU LIKE SQUISH, YOU'LL LOVE BABYMOUSE!

#1 BABYMOUSE: Queen of the World!
#2 BABYMOUSE: Our Hero
#3 BABYMOUSE: Beach Babe
#4 BABYMOUSE: Rock Star
#5 BABYMOUSE: Heartbreaker
#6 CAMP BABYMOUSE
#7 BABYMOUSE: Skater Girl
#8 BABYMOUSE: Puppy Love
#9 BABYMOUSE: Monster Mash
#10 BABYMOUSE: The Musical
#11 BABYMOUSE: Dragonslayer
#12 BABYMOUSE: Burns Rubber
#13 BABYMOUSE: Cupcake Tycoon
#14 BABYMOUSE: Mad Scientist
#15 A Very BABYMOUSE Christmas
#16 BABYMOUSE for President
#17 EXTREME BABYMOUSE
#18 Happy Birthday, BABYMOUSE

And coming soon:

#19 BABYMOUSE: Bad Babysitter

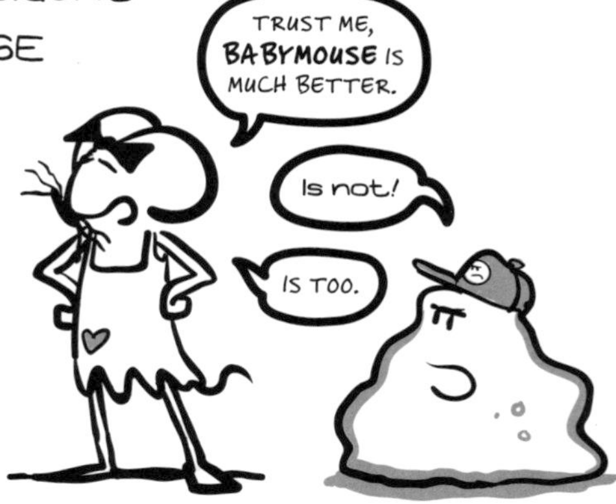
TRUST ME, BABYMOUSE IS MUCH BETTER.
Is not!
IS TOO.

If you like Babymouse,
you'll love these other great books
by Jennifer L. Holm!

THE BOSTON JANE TRILOGY

EIGHTH GRADE IS MAKING ME SICK

THE FOURTEENTH GOLDFISH

MIDDLE SCHOOL IS WORSE THAN MEATLOAF

OUR ONLY MAY AMELIA

PENNY FROM HEAVEN

TURTLE IN PARADISE

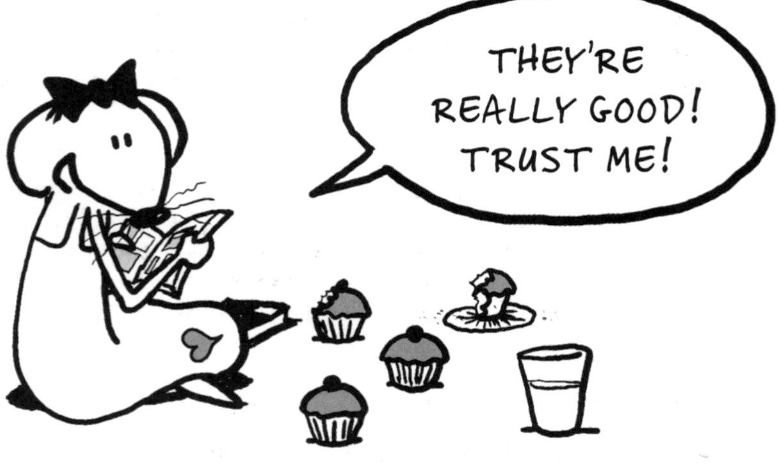
THEY'RE REALLY GOOD! TRUST ME!